Something A

C000134306

L,

e.j.oakes

Prickly-Ink-Press

January: 2022

Thanks to . . .

Mick & Pat
Chris Page
Tim Morris
Antony (Oggy) Ogden
Carol Gane
Tracey Cumbo
Andrew Radley
Andrew (Burt) Reynolds
K.C. Connolly
Paul Peers
Denise Joyce
Trudy Ogden
Yaz Yazinski
Sue Tuke
Geraint Cartwright
Nig Thorpe
Roy (T.V.O.D.) Isherwood
Lisa Callaghan
Gordon Shaw
Kez & Dibber
Sarah Maguire
Sarah Hoskins
Kaz Clinkers
Gaz Hacking
Crissy Worsfold
Mark Hall
Chris Green
Karl Houghton
&
Craig Burton
(Cover Artwork by Airbrush Apocalypse)

The fourth and final area is that of the strongly emergent movement of working-class writing. Silenced for generations, taught to regard literature as a coterie activity beyond their grasp, working people over the past decade in Britain have been actively organizing to find their own literary styles and voices. The workers writers' movement is almost unknown to academia and has not been exactly encouraged by the cultural organs of the state, but it is one sign of a significant break from the dominant relations of literary production.

Terry Eagleton --

Literary Criticism: An Introduction.

If you really want to get people to understand what it is you're doing, do it with a sense of comedy and vague mockery, satire, irony. These are all really, really, useful tools.

- John Lydon

入口: Entrance/Prologue

The mass media serve as a system for communicating messages and symbols to the general populace. It is their function to amuse, entertain, and inform, and to inculcate individuals with the values, beliefs, and codes of behavior that will integrate them into the institutional structures of the larger society. In a world of concentrated wealth and major conflicts of class interest, to fulfill this role requires systematic propaganda.

- Noam Chomsky (Manufacturing Consent)

*

"From roadside signs telling us to 'Stay Alert', the incessantly doom-laden media commentary, to masks literally keeping the fear in our face, we've become afraid of each other. Humans are now vectors of transmission, agents of disease. We have become afraid of our own judgement about how to manage the minutiae of our lives, from who to hug to whether to share a serving spoon. Apparently, we even need guidance about whether we can sit next to a friend on a bench. But perhaps we need to be more afraid of how easily manipulated we can be."
— Laura Dodsworth, A State of Fear: How the UK government weaponised fear during the Covid-19 pandemic

Part A: Other . . .

Falling back headlong to the start of it all, Miles woke up early and regained consciousness to the sound of barking dogs, cursing at them as he shivered and turned over in an attempt to capture a few more minutes sleep, but then remembered that it was payday, and his money would be in the bank. Sat on the edge of his bed, he grabbed the remote to turn on the BBC news and hurried to pull on his jeans and jumper in the frigid Yorkshire air. The narrowboat he was occupying with a friend was always cold at this time of the day he reminded himself, as he first drank the dregs from a can of beer then downed the half glass of wine that was remaining from the previous night between pulling on each of his soiled socks.

Brew.

He needed something warm in his belly, so he lit the gas ring and shook the kettle to see if it contained enough water.

It did.

The walk along the canal to the nearest cashpoint was today accompanied by cawing crows and as usual it was mildly uplifting no matter what the weather and he was thankful that he'd been asked last year to occupy the barge for an old friend who had to return home to Amsterdam due to a family illness. In agreeing to look after the narrowboat, he'd been guaranteed occupancy for at least a year, which had turned into two, and he and his Dutch friend had come to some arrangement whereby he could claim rent from the social for his accommodation which would be paid to his landlady, who would then deposit half of the amount into a second account that Miles had had since forever. It was an amicable arrangement, and one which Miles was thankful for because after lockdown had been implemented and bubbling had become a thing, he was no longer really able to visit his parents over in Bolton and take advantage of the rolls of cash that his father kept stashed in the back of his wardrobe with his "magazines for men".

There was a queue at the cashpoint of a dozen or so people who were stood two meters apart, which made the line appear that much longer, as an overweight uniformed man in his fifties who, Miles assumed, had been employed by the bank to enforce the rule stood nearby. Miles joined the back of the line of atomized and masked individuals who stood invariably looking at a phone as the queue inched toward the machine. He took out his own device, plugged in the earbuds and pulled up a video that he'd watched a couple of times but wanted to see again. The feeling of depression which he'd initially experienced wasn't as intense and he now felt a degree of anger that hadn't rose within him in quite some time. It was a discussion between Roger Hallam, one of the founding members of Extinction Rebellion and Peter Carter, the UN-IPCC expert reviewer, and the outlook wasn't good. Mr. Carter was saying that atmospheric greenhouse gas concentrations were accelerating like never and that recent studies had found that atmospheric carbon dioxide was now the highest in 23 million years: We no longer need to worry about our grandchildren because we now need to be concerned about our children.

Miles could feel a panic attack coming on and opened a different tab and searched for the Extinction Rebellion website to confirm what he already knew because he had to check, just had to, he told himself. He had to read and check in order to confirm because every now and then, he doubted himself, or rather doubted that people could be as stupid as to be so neglectful when it came to something as important as saving the earth that they lived upon. He read –

THIS IS AN EMERGENCY

Life on Earth is in crisis. Our climate is changing faster than scientists predicted and the stakes are high. Biodiversity loss. Crop failure. Social and ecological collapse. Mass extinction. We are running out of time, and our governments have failed to act. Extinction Rebellion was formed to fix this.

Although the weather was overcast and not particularly bright, Miles put on his sunglasses, pulled his masks up high on the bridge of his nose while securing the lower part under his chin and quietly wept, as APONI his spirit guide, swelled with pride.

Some people, he thought to himself, were so damn selfish that it beggared belief at times and he was genuinely astonished that people still used fossil fuels to the degree that they did when everybody knew that it was imperative to switch to wind and solar. On top of that, most people still ate meat and there were even those who refused to wear a mask during a pandemic and still others that were openly opposed to being vaccinated. Climate deniers and pandemic deniers: sheer filth and scum of the earth he was once again telling himself, as the tears began to now soak the upper part of his "anarchy" mask. He'd make himself two or three more later in the day he decided, he had enough black fabric from an old pair of jeans, the anarchy-sign stencil that he'd made and half a pot of fabric paint; it'd give him something to do, take his mind off his problems, the problems created by the deniers and their ilk who were most likely American and had years ago voted for Trump. Well, Trump was gone (thank fuck) and Biden was in, and soon Camila Harris would be in charge, and we'll begin to see some real change, authentic progress from a genuine and bona-fide person of color.

America was the root of all evil and warranted some attention, even though he lived thousands of miles away and had never visited the place, he knew it well. He despised Republicans and although he'd never voted Tory and was vehemently against Boris and Brexit, he'd reluctantly had to concede that Johnson et al had been right to put the country into extended lockdown, enforce social distancing and mask wearing and to push for universal vaccination. Miles just hoped that he wouldn't open-up the country for too long and that the scientists, experts like Neil Ferguson and Matt Hancock, Chris Witty and Sir Patrick Vallance, would lockdown again soon until they were absolutely 100% certain that the pandemic had passed, which it probably never would. Lockdowns had ended way too early, and the irresponsibility of politicians baffled him because not only were they useful in flattening the curve when it came to the coronavirus, they had also shown to reduce the amount of carbon dioxide being released into the atmosphere as people stayed home and towns and cities fell largely silent.

Miles wished with all his heart that the government would do something more, something substantive and sustainable about the climate crisis, from which he was sure, was born the cov-19 pandemic. Miles hated America and all Americans, every last one of them he'd often tell people, though he did love the San Francisco punk band Dead Kennedys and the L.A. based Bad Religion: Eco-friendly bands with a real purpose, a cause worthy of adoration and respect; spiritual, life-affirming and rebellious.

The line to the cash machine was starting to move and once it had come to a stop again, Miles pulled down his mask a little and wiped his eyes with his coat sleeve: It was just that he cared so much for the planet, the animals and nature. It was just that he so despised humanity and its disregard for common sense and the notion of universal equity, opportunity, and respect. His mind wandered to Jello Biafra and his remarks about extreme weather conditions, and he began to involuntarily silently sob and once again wiped his eyes with his sleeve before switching his masks around. Miles was, as usual, double masked, just to be on the safe side; to keep himself safe and to protect others should he happen to contract any coronavirus variant that rendered him asymptomatic and well, to show that he cared. Miles was a really caring person he told himself, and he made every attempt each day to let others around him see this, which he was certain would endear himself toward them.

Miles hated all Americans, and he was proud of it, though he did love Dead Kennedys, Bad Religion and . . .

. . . *and me,* interrupted APONI his spirit guide.

'Of course,' Miles silently replied. 'And you.'

He'd often wondered why it was an American that had entered his spiritual life to guide him through the nocuous labyrinth of the wicked modern world, but it all made sense one night when he was at a particularly low ebb, that APONI had visited him and revealed that she was Native American, which isn't *really* American at all Miles assured himself, not one bit. "APONI" was the Native American (Pima) word for *butterfly* and Miles had got himself one tattooed just below his beltline, just above his pubic region.

It then began to rain, and Miles stood close to the wall in a partially successful attempt to avoid getting a drenching, as several people in front of him in the queue decided that getting soaked wasn't worth whatever transaction they were aiming to attend to at the cashpoint.

There were now only three people ahead of him and he felt his heart leap as the woman just having finished her business at the machine turned as she tucked her card and cash into the pockets of her purse before looking up the road through the rain and past Miles as she walked in his direction.

'Tilly?' asked Miles as she approached where he was stood, squinting through the sudden English downpour as she herself opened an umbrella. 'Matilda Burns?'

'Excuse me?' she replied, turning as she passed where he was stood. 'Have we met before?'

'It's me Tilly, Miles,' he said, pulling down his masks. 'Miles Beta.'

∞

'I'm sorry I didn't recognize you Miles,' said Tilly, flushed a little with embarrassment, as he lit the gas to make some tea before taking a seat with her at the small table. 'How long has it been?'

'M'not sure,' he replied. 'Thirty, thirty-five years, more?'

♩ *flick'd a match into my brain* . . . sang APONI.

'Nottingham right, Forest Fields yeah?'

'Yeah, well almost. I was living in a flat on Gregory Boulevard with your cousin.'

'*How* is Ray? Where *is* Ray?'

'He's here in Hebden,' replied Miles, a degree of anxiety now suddenly obvious as the foot of his crossed leg began to slowly and slightly but noticeably bounce, as though to an unheard melody.

'And how is he, is he ok?'

'Will be when she's finally made the transition,' replied Miles, aware of the hollow ring at the feminine pronoun he'd prematurely chosen to use. 'He will be.'

'Why,' asked Tilly, 'where's he going? He emigrating?'

'I'll let him explain,' said Miles. 'I'll give you his number, you can phone him, he won't be back for another day or two, maybe three.'

'No Miles,' replied Tilly in a friendly manner that conveyed her desire not to put either him or her cousin to any trouble. 'I don't need his number; I wouldn't know what to say. I know he's my cousin, but we've never been close. I don't know him in all honesty and have probably only ever exchanged a handful of words with him. I've only ever seen him about six times and that was mostly when we were kids. Nah, I don't want to call him, it'd only be awkward.'

Miles said: 'He's proud to be your cousin if I'm honest, likes to be associated with you and your achievements somehow.'

'Achievements?'

'Well,' replied Miles, his foot still nervously dancing, 'I think you were the only one of us that started at uni around the same time who went on to do a PhD.'

'There wasn't much work around at the time Miles love, so I decided to just continue studying in the hope that sometime later down the line I would be able to find a job. It was a lot easier then, I mean more affordable and not like now with kids being priced out of being able to attend university, even if they've got the grades and the inclination.'

'So what did you study exactly? Was it biology?'

'Ecology in the end, though I started off with Forestry: I was a tree-hugger back then if you remember: peace-punk, hippie, dreadlocks, vegan earth-child . . .

'Save the whale . . .

'Acid rain,' replied Tilly.

'Do they owe us a living?' beamed Miles, recalling their bastardized middle-class student-days routine from decades earlier.

'Of course,' they chorused. 'Of course they ruddy do.'

'We were so dorky,' laughed Tilly. 'Weak and ineffectual: "Of course they ruddy do"?'

'How so?' asked Miles as he stood, before asking, 'D'you want some toast?'

'Yeah, toast would be nice. What I mean is, we had to dilute everything with our middle-class sensibilities; reduce the word FUCKING as an expletive to RUDDY because we thought we knew better, believed we were more perceptive than what we sometimes referred to as the "chanting-chimps" from the council estates with their enthusiasm for Crass on the one hand or Exploited on the other. We were interlopers Miles when it came to being punks in the early eighties. Good laugh though,' she laughed. 'Met some people that I would have never expected to when I was growing up in Bromley Cross and Edgerton.'

Miles creased his brow quizzically, as he often did, rather than say anything that may make him appear even remotely disagreeable, particularly given present company. Miles very much saw himself as a punk, a peace punk, an anarcho-vegan punk and not now and not ever an interloper. Members of Crass were middle-class and he'd been brought up middle-class: So what? So what if he sometimes ate eggs. What was the problem in him eating pizza from time to time? He was still a vegan. Theoretically.

'You disagree?' asked Tilly teasing his awkwardness.

Miles' mood began to lift a little at the thought that Tilly might be flirting with him with her teasing, but he did his best to hide his feelings and imagined that he was concealing intellectual amusement behind the smile he couldn't hide. After all, he'd once began a degree in Sociology, so was somewhat qualified to comment on social class and examples of its cultural manifestations such as punk.

'I think you're hinting at class, but I don't see class,' he said suddenly feeling more confident of himself, now realizing and recalling, remembering that Tilly wasn't the kind of person to judge him, he didn't like to be judged. 'I just see people; we're all the same.'

'Maybe,' she replied with a smile as she passed him the loaf of bread that was behind her on a shelf along with a tobacco tin and a few tattered paperbacks.

'Thanks,' he said before asking, 'Maybe?'

'Maybe we're all the same deep down at the core of our humanity and the fact that we all breath in oxygen and exhale CO_2, but when it comes to countries, cultures and social classes I think that there are innumerable differences which sometimes click together and at others clash.'

♮ - 'And I believe in this,' quietly sang APONI, 'and it's been tested by research . . .

'So how are we ever going to make the world a better place if people continue to clash and our differences aren't solved?'

. . . he who fucks nuns, will later join the church.' - ♪

'You're not going to make the world a better place, are you?' she smiled again.

Her smile was contagious, and Miles enjoyed it: 'But we have to try though, right?'

'The problem is,' she replied, 'is that everybody is trying in different ways, there's no one concerted effort to "make the world a better place" as you say. The best you can do is improve your own world and leave everyone else alone to organize their own little world and put things in order the way they see fit.'

'Peanut butter?' he asked. 'Or margarine.'

As she sat spreading peanut butter on her toast, Miles replied, 'But there are a lot of people who just don't care, who can't really be trusted to live a responsible life.'

'Can't really be trusted?'

'No, people who don't recycle and continue to eat meat. People who have no regard for Mother Nature, the planet.'

'Such as?' she asked.

'*Most people*!' he exclaimed, though with a smile that he hoped would help to engender some degree of affable concurrence. 'Humanity is a plague.'

'Some people care,' said Tilly, 'or least claim to. There are a lot of people who feel the same way that you do.'

'Such as?' he asked.

'Extinction Rebellion claim to care.'

'And you think they don't?'

'Do you?' replied Tilly.

'Well actually,' said Miles. 'I think they do; yeah, of course they do. In fact,' he continued, as he spread butter on his own toast and nodded towards a pile of bunting on a bench further down the narrowboat, 'I've been working on a project for one of their events later this year, maybe next.'

'Oh yeah?'

'Yeah. Some members of a local group from Halifax or somewhere came into Hebden and did a funky flash-mob last year and I found it really inspiring, so did Pez.'

'Pez?'

'Sorry, Periwinkle.'

'Periwinkle?' asked Tilly.

'Your Ray, she goes by Periwinkle or Pez these days.

'So that's what you meant by transitioning?'

'Yeah, it is yeah,' he replied as he handed her a plate. 'D'you wanna another brew?'

'Yeah, go on then, if you're having one,' said Tilly as she leaned in and kissed Miles on the cheek: 'Good to see you again Miles love; what a nice surprise, so glad to know you're happy and well and living in such a beautiful place, You deserve nothing less, I'm made up for you.'

2

Periwinkle Burns was on her way back to Hebden after attending a workshop for direct action that'd been held in Derby over the past three days and was aimed specifically at trans-women, when she bumped into an acquaintance she hadn't seen in almost as long as Miles hadn't seen Tilly. She'd planned to stay at the workshop two or three days longer but excused herself saying that she was beginning to have panic attacks being in town around so many people, some of whom weren't even masked. Her comrades said that they understood, wished her well and said that they hoped to see her sometime in the future when she was feeling better and could make it to a demo. As she was approaching the coach station in Sheffield after the train ride over from Derby, she called into a nearby corner shop to buy a can of larger or two for the trip back to the narrowboat and exiting as she was entering was Frank, she recognized him immediately.

'Frank mate: Bolts from the Bolton days?'

'Yeah?'

'It's me mate, Ray. Blister.'

'It *is* too, how're you doing pal: long see no time eh – Jesus.'

As it turned out, Bolts too was heading over to Hebden, so the two naturally chose to travel together: In fact, it wasn't even a choice, it was simply a welcome coincidence that was acknowledged and laughed at. The pair, along with Tilly and Miles, had been part of a large group of teens and twenty-somethings which made up the Bolton punk scene in the initial half of the eighties. Bolts and Ray Burns, a.k.a. Blister, had even been part of the same extended group of a dozen-or-so punks that occupied a couple of flats a short ten-minute walk out of town. They hadn't been close friends, though having been part of the same group they shared a few good memories of the two or three years they spent in each other's nearby orbit. Miles and Tilly on the other hand had been a year or two younger and in sixth form readying themselves for university in Nottingham. Blister, along with a handful of others also moved over to Nottingham and he even registered as an art student, which was more about the grant than any kind of qualification, life direction or ambition. He dropped out after the first term and worked part-time in a wholefood shop where he drove the delivery van, and a year or so later, Miles quit his sociology degree and rather than go back to Bolton shame-faced with his tail between his legs to his disappointed parents, he too got a job at the same wholefood shop, which is how he and Ray became close friends. Miles was one of a trio that made vegan pasties and other savories and Ray delivered them to various shops around town which had agreed to sell their goods on a sale or return basis in exchange for a nominal commission.

Frank, a.k.a. Bolts, didn't comment on Blister's outfit as they sat at the back of the coach and opened a beer apiece as it pulled out of the station: The pink canvas Converse footwear, the lime-green colored tights, the thigh-length tight black skirt, the tie-dye sweatshirt beneath the kaki German military jacket. He'd been gone awhile (multiple decades) and acknowledged to himself that he was out of the loop when it came to middle-aged vegan punks and what these days passed for anarcho-chic. It wasn't the clothes as much as it was the bald head and the grey beard and the greying shoulder length hair at the back which on either side was twisted into some type of proto-dreadlock and held in place by a small bow made from dirty yellow ribbon.

It wasn't so much the clothes as it was the hair, and it wasn't so much the hair as it was the camp intonation that years ago wasn't there, the Larry Grayson act: "Shut that door."

'So where've you been Bolts love? Not seen *you* in decades.'

'Nice anarchy mask,' replied Bolts. 'Where d'you get that?'

'Miles made it; he's got a sewing machine.'

'Oh yeah, you still see Miles.'

'Lived together for years in one place or another,' said Blister, lowering his mask to take a mouthful of beer before replacing it and remarking, 'You're supposed to keep your mask on in a closed environment, the driver will throw you off if he sees you've removed your mask.'

'I'll just keep out sight then,' said Bolts, as he further hunkered down on the back seat in the corner next to the window. 'Let us know if for any reason he decides to head this way.'

'I don't think he can see you, but somebody getting on the bus might notice you're not wearing a mask and tell him.'

'You don't have to wear them these days.'

'Do,' said Periwinkle, a.k.a. Pez, a.k.a. Blister. 'Yeah we do.'

'Better sit on the other side then,' said Bolts, as he put on his mask before squeezing past Blister so that he could sit on the opposite side, the driver's side.

'So,' said Bolts. 'Am I right in thinking that you're wearing a bra?'

'That's a bit insensitive isn't it, a little direct?'

'Fuck off Blister; knock it off eh and tell us what's going on yeah?'

Ray Burns a.k.a. Blister was a big fella and Periwinkle a.k.a. Pez is a big lass, but not large enough to get too touchy with Bolts, a.k.a., Frank Norman Stein. Blister knew from days gone by that his old acquaintance here wasn't at all shy of conflict and that being bigger wasn't necessarily in this present context an advantage, as was often the case. There'd been rumors, talk of Frank and his escapades, one of which involved a pair of tin-snips. Frank, or Bolts as he was more commonly known, had been sharing a flat with a couple of other punks, one of which had taken pity on a lad younger than themselves. By this time Bolts and his mates must have been in their early twenties, whereas this lad had just turned eighteen and was homeless, penniless, and cared for little other than sniffing glue. He'd stayed at the flat for a few days until he hooked up with a couple of other punks who lived down the road who had moved over from Westhoughton. On the day that he'd packed his carrier bag and walked down the street to his new place, the lad had decided to take Bolts' turntable which had led him looking to retrieve it. After discovering that the younger fella had indeed took the turntable, Bolts had given him a clobbering, sat on his chest and pinned the lad's arms down with his knees before sticking the tinsnips up one nostril and leaving a nigh on inch-long snick as a way of illustrating that such thievery after showing generosity would not be tolerated, under any fuckin' circumstances. At least, that was the rumor.

'What if I am wearing a bra?'

'Why are you wearing a bra when you've got no tits?'

Periwinkle was deeply hurt and felt the need for a safe-space where she could curl up and hide but of course there was no safe-space on the bus, she had to conjure up a bit of maturity and sit with her own feelings for a while as she explained: 'Ray and Blister are names I no longer use Bolts,' said Periwinkle. 'My name now is Periwinkle or Pez for short.'

'Periwinkle?' asked Bolts. 'Like the flower?'

'Like the flower: Yes, like the flower.'

'Sounds mard to me mate, you big girl's blouse: what're you like eh? Jesus. And anyhow, you just introduced yourself to me as Ray and Blister back there at shop, you big daft knob.'

'Toxic masculinity that is Bolts,' replied Periwinkle a she lowered her gaze. 'If I'm honest.'

'Oh aye,' laughed Frank. 'And other platitudes.'

'Whatever d'you mean, platitudes?'

'Overly used phrases that you've been nudged into accepting, internalizing and repeating.'

'*How* so?' asked Periwinkle.

'How *so*?' asked Frank.

'Yeah. Are you trying to suggest that someone else has influenced my thinking? Because I can assure Bolts, that is not the case.'

'Yeah it is,' said Bolts. 'You've bought the yarn mate, hook, line and sinker. You've internalized the narrative and now you're part of it, like most punks mate. No wonder they're laughing.'

'How so?' repeated Periwinkle, acting up by feigning faux outrage. 'Prove it.'

'Okay,' replied Bolts as he leant over and the two tapped beer cans. 'Cheers, and no hard feelings.'

'So how are you going to prove it?' asked Pez, slightly relieved.

Frank stuck his can on the floor and held it upright between his feet and fished about in a backpack until he found a pen, a small pad of post-it notes and a book. He then peeled five notes from the pad and wrote a couple of words on the back-side of each of them before sticking them on the book in a row blank-side up: He then numbered them one to five.

'What're you doing?' asked Periwinkle.

'Right,' said Frank, 'I'm going to say three or four words and I'd like you to finish the sentence, okay?'

'Okay,' smirked Periwinkle, 'but I'm not sure what you're expecting.'

'Just say what you think, but keep it simple, three or four words okay?'

'Okay.'

'Okay, first one. You ready?'

'I'm ready.'

'Right,' said Bolts. 'Number one: climate change is an . . .

'Existential threat?' replied Periwinkle.

'That's right yeah, just say what you think, what makes most sense to you.'

'Now what?'

'Number two,' said Frank. 'Tommy Robinson is a . . .

'Fuckin' racist,' replied Pez.

'Okay, number three of five. Islam is . . .

'A religion of peace.'

'Number four. Donald Trump is a . . .

'Orange fascist . . .

'And the last one,' said Frank. 'Katie Hopkins is . . .

'A right-wing whore.'

'Okay,' said Frank, offering the book and the post-it notes to Pez after they once again tapped beers cans. 'Peel off number one and read what it says on the back will you?'

Pez peeled off the first post-it, turned it over and read: 'Existential threat.'

Frank wrote a few words on a sixth post-it before asking: 'You think so?'

'Of course I do.'

'Why?'

'Because ninety-seven percent of all scientists think it's an existential threat.'

Frank turned the sixth post-it around and held it up: It read –

97% of all scientists.

'Ready for number two?' asked Frank.

'Go on then,' replied Pez. 'Turn it over.'

'*You* turn it over.'

Pez removed the second post-it from the book which sat on the back seat of the coach between the two of them and read: 'Racist.'

'Number three,' said Bolts, and Pez turned over the third post-it and read: 'Religion of peace.'

'The fourth one now.'

'I'm not liking this if I'm honest,' said Periwinkle a.k.a. Pez, in what Frank a.k.a. Bolts, thought was a whining tone before reading: 'Fascist.'

'And the last one.'

'It says, far-right slag. But that's not what I said; I said right-wing whore.'

'Big difference,' laughed Bolts as he finished the last of what was in the can before scrunching it up, sticking it in a plastic carrier bag and placing it in the net pocket that was screwed to the back of the seat in front of him.

'But what does any of that mean Bolts? It doesn't really prove anything does it?'

'It proves that despite the anarchy sign on your mask there and the "Fuck the System" tattoo that I suspect you still have on your left arm, that you hold the same views as the Tories in Downing Street, the twats of Fleet Street and their ilk, and those just like them on-line. You are the system mate. You've been nudged into holding the opinions that you believe in, and your thinking is predictable, as we've just illustrated.'

'I don't agree,' said Pez. 'I'm not that easily influenced.'

'That's what all captured minds say,' said Bolts, as he opened his second can as he hummed a brief line of a song to himself and sarcastically winked at a visibly irritated Pez: 'M-m-m-m-m-m-m-m/m . . . ♪

3.

'And when did he decide that he wanted to, as you say, transition?' asked Tilly, as Miles sat cutting a piece of black cloth that he intended to hem before attaching pieces of cord that would hook behind his ears. In all honesty, he rather liked working with the needle and cotton in front of Tilly, he assumed it made him look like a modern male; sensitive, in touch with his feminine side and progressive: artistic too – talented.

Tilly sat and wondered why Miles didn't buy a cheap box of disposable masks if he was really that concerned about contracting a virus, as she believed that any attempt to prevent a virus from passing through the material that he was using was similar to using a sieve to stop rain. Maybe he wasn't too concerned about the virus and was just avoiding unnecessarily spending any money on something he thought served no realistic function, perhaps he was just going along to get along and chose to wear a face-covering to avoid the spiteful wrath of other people and to be able to do his shopping and errands without attracting any negative attention. So why then, she thought to herself, was he wearing two masks when she bumped into him earlier at the bank? Why on earth was he *still* wearing two masks?

'Well,' replied Miles, 'I suppose it's been two or three years, maybe four, m'not sure really.'

'Really?'

'Really.'

'And when d'you say he'll be back?'

'Not sure, I'll text him.'

'No Miles love, you don't have to, I haven't seen him in years, decades in fact and . . .

'I'll just ask him when he thinks he'll be back and mention that I saw you outside the bank this morning, that all.'

Miles put aside his sewing for the moment, a little miffed that his sewing machine was out of order, and focused his attention on the phone which sat on the small table as he began to roll a cigarette, while Tilly stood to stretch her legs and look around the vessel. They were sat in the fore-well at the front of the narrowboat and she mouthed, out of pointless politeness, 'Can I have a quick look around?'

Miles smiled and nodded, 'Mi casa, es su casa.'

The section next to the fore-well was the kitchen area or galley and beyond that toward the aft was a toilet and shower, then a double bed, then another toilet, then another sleeping area with a single bed on either side. The boat could accommodate four very easily, six at a squeeze. Tilly imagined life on the canals to be quite comfortable, idyllic even, given the scenery and the optimism of a mild English winter and perhaps someday soon, a day or two of sunshine. The boat was ample sized really, and roomier than several apartments she'd lived in over the years on her travels, though the décor, familiar as it was, somehow churned her stomach with jaded nostalgia and a past that she'd grown away from years ago. The weathered and tatty punk posters which occupied each available flat surface seemed to haunt her in a manner which only echoed through the years, back to her own naivety and distinct lack of nuance when it came to processing the political climate of the day. She sat looking at the Angelic Upstarts promotional poster for *Teenage Warning*, their first album, reckoning that it was over forty years old, older than many people she'd known who had died before they'd reached that age, or even thirty for that matter. She searched for a while inside herself to see *what* exactly irritated her about these soiled images of the past and found the answer to be simple really: It was the shabbiness of it all. Not the shoddiness of it then in the late seventies when a song like *Teenage Warning* was bellowed from the lungs of a young Mensi in his early twenties to the ears of an audience of pre-twenty-somethings, but the gimcrack appeal it still had for fellas fast approaching sixty. Moreover, the apparent unwillingness to put any of it into a twenty-first century perspective, to show any kind of interest in wrestling with the subtleties of ideological merit.

'Y'okay?' asked Miles as he entered the aft-end sleeping area. 'You look lost.'

'Just doing a bit of silent reminiscing love,' she replied without looking at him, still staring glassy-eyed at the poster.

'What,' he laughed, 'over an Angelic Upstarts poster?'

'I used to listen to that album a lot when I was a teenager, our John got it for his birthday, August 1979.'

'I never really liked it myself, replied Miles. 'To *Oi!* for my liking if you know what I mean.'

'Out before *Oi!*, if I remember rightly.'

'Well, you know what I mean. I just put it up there to brighten the place up, make the place look the part because I don't wanna live on a tourist looking boat, there're enough of them wandering up and down the canals these days, though not as many over the past year and more due to the coronavirus.'

'I was just wondering what Mensi might think of all this, you know, whether or not he's changed his tune any or refined his ideas at all.'

'Refined his ideas?' asked Miles, scoffing a little at the notion, but not too much, to avoid irritating Tilly.

'Like Sham 69 they were and sometimes are accused of being a racist skinhead band they were if I rightly recall, lumped in with the NF at times, when in actual fact they were always left-leaning and vocal supporters of anti-fascism.'

'So how come you're wondering whether or not they've, as you say, refined their ideas? I'm not with you?'

'Well,' said Tilly. 'Like I say, I remember them supporting an anti-fascist movement back in the day and . . .

'Didn't we all?' asked Miles.

'Didn't we all what?'

'Didn't we all support anti-fascist movements?'

'Of course we did, but that's not really my point Miles love.'

'So, what is your point?' asked Miles, unaware that Tilly could easily detect the lascivious interest that lined the fabricated curiosity of his question.

'Mensi and the Upstarts and all of us were and always have been anti-fascist and Mensi and the Upstarts and myself, I don't know about you Miles, have always been anti-communist as well but . . .

'I'm not anti-communist,' Miles interjected. 'Are you?'

'Another conversation that is love,' she replied. 'Later. The thing is, these days, ANTIFA are solemn bedmates with BLM who are self-confessed trained communists, so I was sat here wondering how, if at all, Mensi and the Upstarts had refined their ideas to accommodate this obviously awkward relationship and the fact he has said he is against using violence to further a cause, and yet ANTIFA have no reservations in doing so.'

'You're joking?' said Miles, unsure of how to proceed. 'Really?'

'ANTIFA in L.A. showed up at a protest and got violent in support of a transgender woman who, in a spa-space designated for females, decided to show off his junk in front of women and girls. So, although Mensi and co are in favor of anti-fascism, I'm not quite sure they'd be in support of that particular ANTIFA chapter and such idiotic wokery as labeling a woman who complained about a man flashing his tally-wacker and love spuds in front of her daughter, as a fascist.'

'You're joking,' Miles repeated, without clarifying which side of the fence he was sat on.

'Many a true word said in jest,' she replied, wanting to avoid a knotty conversation. 'And anyhow, that album's far more interesting,' she said pointing at a promotional poster for their second album, *We Gotta Get Out of This Place*.

'Never heard it,' said Miles acting slightly nonplussed.

'But that, that there is my favorite,' enthused Tilly pointing over at a black and white poster. 'Always been my favorites.'

'One of my favorite bands ever, know the words to all their songs, yet I never saw them live, did you?'

'I did yeah, half a dozen or more times,' she said before pausing in thought. 'I tell you what, you put the kettle on and make us another brew and roll us a joint yeah? You do still have a smoke, don't you?'

The two made their way back to the fore-well at the front of the boat where Tilly sat at the table looking in her backpack for the small waterproof camping bag that she used to store the tin which contained her smoking tackle, while Miles stood behind her in the kitchen area making more tea.

'I sent a text to Pez but she hasn't got back to me yet,' he said.

'Pez?'

'Periwinkle: Ray, your cousin.'

'Oh, yeah, right. You shouldn't have bothered Miles love; like I say, I haven't seen him in decades and I doubt I'll be around when he does get back.'

'Where're you heading?'

'I'm going back to Bolton for my aunt's funeral. She's been in a care-home with dementia for the past few months and last week she finally passed away, so I dropped everything and flew back.'

'From British Columbia?'

'No, I've been in Texas for the past few months to be closer to the girls: Carla's nineteen now and Jane's twenty; they're both in university down there and well, things haven't been going too well between me and their dad and we decided to split up, it was inevitable really.'

'Oh yeah?' asked Miles, suddenly inwardly illuminated as he took a seat at the table across from her as she put the tin on the table.

'Spliff or pipe?' she asked.

'Hash or weed?' he replied.

'Either.'

'A spliff of hash then if you don't mind, I can't do skunk.'

'Anyhow, his work as a microbiologist has had him out in the field for weeks at a time over the past several years and it turns out he's had a thing going with a colleague of his for the last five or six years, and so we decided to go our own ways. I mean, he's been good with the house and the kids and everything. He' s a good man, it's just that we grew apart from each other, as people do at times.'

'And where is he now?'

'We've sold our place in B.C. and he's taking care of the last few things that need sorting before moving down to L.A. in a month or two.'

'And you?'

'I'll go back to Texas in a month or so to see the girls, then I'm going to Washington D.C. to start a new job,' replied Tilly, as she handed Miles a photograph of her two cheerful looking daughters out shopping.

'They like shopping?' asked Miles.

'They're young girls Miles love, or should I say young women, of course they like shopping.'

'Teaching?' asked Miles as he studied the image. 'Is your husband Asian?'

'Yeah,' replied Tilly. 'Hong Kong Chinese (same as his now partner) but raised in Singapore and moved to Canada when he was eleven, and no - it's a research position with an NGO.'

'But Texas, why? I mean America: awful place.'

'You don't like America?' asked Tilly.

'*Eeew*, no.'

'Or Americans?'

'No: *eeew*.'

Just then Miles' phone signaled that he'd received a message and the kettle in the kitchen began to whistle, so he stood looking at the screen and went to take care of the tea as Tilly sat back, put the pipe to her lips and inhaled a long lung-full of THC before rolling a spliff for Miles who was now talking on the phone somewhere away from the kitchen and toward the aft. Tilly sat with the pipe in her hand and once again thought of the yellowing poster back there and the eternal anguish that seemed to envelop Britain in regard to inherent yet largely unseen, though ever present anxiety. She did honestly wonder what the Upstarts thought of ANTIFA and whether the band or any of its members agreed with the methodology that the black-bloc employed, their tactics all the more tolerated, particularly in America, by left-leaning idealogues in prominent positions. She recalled that last year BLM were allowed to protest in London, yet other groups protesting *against* lockdowns and *for* their civil liberties were met with fierce resistance from a police force controlled by Ms. Dick and Mr. Khan.

Did the band approve of the police - whom they have accused of being fascists - coming down hard on working-class anti-lockdown protestors, while turning a blind eye to the largely middle-class Extinction Rebellion folk closing down parts of the city and supergluing themselves to anything that caught their eye.

'I'll just put the kettle on again Tilly,' said Miles suddenly appearing and handing her a rolled-up poster. 'Here,' he smiled, 'you can have this, seeing as you like it so much.'

'Oh,' said Tilly, suddenly surprised. 'Thanks.'

'Just turned the kettle off while I spoke to Pez; did you roll a spliff?'

'I did yeah,' she said, as she heard Miles switch the gas back on and the sound of cups and spoons begin to clatter.

Frank sat watching the scenery slide by as Pez, who'd wandered down to the middle of the coach to an unoccupied seat, sat talking on the phone. It'd been a year or more, nigh on eighteen months now, since his father had died and he'd been unable to make it back to the U.K. for the funeral due to the fact that he'd have had to quarantine for two weeks on arrival and would have missed the ceremony anyway, so he'd watched the funeral unfold live online as he sat up around midnight thousands of miles away. Then, there was the possibility that he wouldn't be able to reenter Japan: Citizens and residents were allowed back in, but Frank only had temporary residency at the time and was aware that things were changing by the day. His concern was that he might leave when the rules permitted temporary residents to return, only to have them change while he was away to restrict reentry to citizens and permanent residents only. He didn't want to find himself trapped in the U.K. because he had nowhere to stay. Like Tilly, he'd been gone a long time and people were scared. Most of his friends were following the Tory rules and bubbling, afraid that if they interacted with "outsiders" they would contract the disease and pass it on to elderly, more vulnerable relatives. The propaganda on the posters warned: *Stay Home, Don't Kill Grandma*, or some such shite.

The, "Don't Kill Grandma" mantra had been cooked up by some government nudge-department or other in order to frighten the population into following the covid-19 regulations and as far as Frank could see, it had been effective.

"TV invents a disease you think . . . 🎼

Bad news for baldies as new US study finds they are 40% more at risk of coronavirus

- *Daily Star,* **23 July 2020**

Mat Hancock wars the whole population is at risk o 'long Covid'

- *Daily Mail,* **17 November 2020**

Boris Johnson fights 'truly frightening' virus as Michael Gove tells of Cabinet shock at PM's condition

-   *Evening Standard*, **7 April 2020**

Don't go out and enjoy the sunshine

-   *The Daily Telegraph*, **4 April 2020**

Covid 'could damage fertility of up to 20% of male survivors'

-   *Metro*, **12 November 2020**

Is testicle pain potentially a sign of Covid? 49-year-old Turkish man who had no other symptoms is diagnosed with the virus

-   *Mail Online*, **18 November 2020**

Baby left with lifelong condition after developing rare syndrome linked to coronavirus

-   *Wales Online*, **15 November 2020**

COVID-19 could cause erectile dysfunction in patients who have recovered from the virus, doctor warns

-   *Daily Mail*, **6 November 2020**

Health officials recommend 'glory holes' for safe sex during pandemic - *Metro*, **23 July 2020**

. . . you have. ♪

The media had subtle and undeniable clout and Bolts had these punk mates that, like many well-known punk musicians, were clamoring to be vaccinated so that they could get back out there into the pubs and clubs, enjoy the company of their pals and live music again. Some of them expressed their desire online to slap those who refused to wear a mask in public, no matter how far away from other people, and there were those who accused folk not wanting to be vaccinated as being paranoid due to having smoked too much weed in the past. Bolts, on the other hand, believed it was they who were unnecessarily afraid of a virus which had a recovery rate of over ninety-nine percent for those under the age of seventy-five or thereabouts. The average age of death from covid was reported to be around eighty-two, while the average lifespan anyway was a year or so younger. Something was going on it seemed to Bolts, though he knew not specifically what . . .

♮ – *Nobody knows, nobody cares . . .*

There were too many inconsistencies which only ever seemed to suggest that Boris and his mates were either incompetent or malicious, he hoped the former was the case rather than the latter. A few short months prior to the announcement that there was a pandemic, a lot of Frank's anarcho-punk pals had been screeching all manner of insults in the direction of Boris Johnson as he wrestled to finalize Brexit in Britain's favor. They said that to be pro-Brexit was to be patriotic, and to have any kind of respect for a national flag that represented a nation state with borders was to be xenophobic and racist, a fascist to be despised and shunned. Yet here they were, many of them were busy . . .

"*Looking at the numbers . . . ♮*

. . . and vehemently urging *Mr. Politician* Boris to lockdown tighter and for longer, implement more stringent regulations regarding masking, social distancing, and vaccinations, because *they* wanted to hurry up and get back down the pub. Say NO, the punks say, to national I.D. cards, because they are an affront to individual liberty they say, and say YES to international digital vaccine passports because they are the key to communal freedom.

'Just spoke to Miles,' said Pez as she retook her seat. 'You'll never guess who's with him at the boat?'

'At the boat?'

'We live on a narrowboat that we've rented from a Dutch friend who had to go back to Amsterdam. It's Miles' place really but he lets' me gum & co as I please.'

'Oh yeah?' said Frank, inwardly amused and somewhat surprised that Pez or Periwinkle or Blister or Ray or whatever he was called these days had the same linguistic tick. 'Sounds good. You get about on it or d'you just stay put?'

'We don't travel too much, though we have made one or two trips over to Rochdale and Bolton.

'Sounds good,' he said again.

'So anyhow, guess who's at the boat with Miles.'

'No idea mate.'

'GUESS!'

'Are you telling us or what?' asked Frank.

'Tilly: My cousin Tilly!'

'I didn't know she was your cousin.'

'Well, distant cousin, not first cousins.'

'Not seen her in decades mate, she went to British Columbia in Canada, didn't she?'

'I think so.'

'So how long have you lived on a boat?' asked Frank.

'A few months now, over a year.'

'Right.'

'Where have you been living?'

Frank explained the situation and elaborated a little, outlining how he'd been to see his father's widow in Matlock and after seeing an old friend was on his way to Hebden to pick up a mountain bike that he intended to take back to Japan with him in a couple or three weeks or so. He'd bought the bike cheap from a mate – last time he'd been in Britain – who'd fallen on hard times when his wife had kicked him out of the house. Frank had paid five-hundred quid for the bike and to replace it with a new one of the same quality would cost him more than five times the amount, so going out of his way for a day or two while he was back in England seemed worth his while. His intent was to collect the bike, which when last he saw it was packed up in a travel bag, do any maintenance work on it that was needed, and then ride on over to Bolton where he'd stay on the allotment behind another friend's house near Todmorden. From there he intended and use the bike to go visit any family and still other friends in different parts of Bolton, Leigh, Tyldesley and Atherton who weren't shit-scared of contact with people from outside any covid bubble they may still be observing.

'Really?' mewed Periwinkle. 'Japan! Fancy that will you? And are you working over there?'

'I got a job as a corporate consultant, which basically involves working with company junior executives who are being groomed for more senior positions. They have to go overseas for a period, usually three to five years, and while they're over there they have to enroll in an executive degree course at places like Harvard. So, I go along, and we meet in their office and we read business case studies and discuss them in the same manner that they'll be required to do when they get over there and need to interact with other junior executives from around the world who are enrolled on the same program.'

'Bloody hell Bolts, the last job I recall you having was collecting scrap metal in that Transit van with them two skinheads . . .

'Did that for a while for a few extra quid while I were signing on yeah . . .

'Bloody hell. Anyway, d'you wanna come and say hello to Miles and Tilly, see the boat?'

'Need to pick this bike up first and then head on over to Bolton, but maybe, yeah if I have enough time. You got a phone?'

'Yeah.'

'You on Farcebook?'

'I am yeah,' replied Pez.

'Sound,' said Bolts. 'I'll drop you a line on Mess-engineer when I know what the crack is yeah?'

'Why do you say Farcebook?' asked Pez.

'Because along with Twatter and many of the other big platforms, they agreed from the get-go to get in bed with the politicians and begin to censor any kind of analysis of the pandemic that didn't conform with the official line. A few short years back I was able to spend time on there and keep in touch with friends, but it's different now. Out of almost three hundred friends that I have on there, only about six to ten regularly show up on my News Feed. The rest of what shows up are advertisements, posts from any group I'm in or suggestions of groups I might be interesting in joining. Basically, it's the illusion of interacting with your friends while in reality your interests, likes & dislikes, hobbies & interests, location, age and on and on are being data mined. They're like fuckin' comic vultures mate, pretending that they're impartial. And this neo-new-age gig they've got lined up is farcical, this Meta lark they've got lined up. Jesus.'

The trip from Sheffield Pond Street to Halifax took almost two hours and a couple of cans, so after relieving themselves they spent the next three-quarters-of-an hour dozing off the ale until they arrived at Burnley Road in Hebden where they exchanged contact details, shared an awkward pally back-slapping hug, and went their separate ways.

5

'So why Hebden?' asked Miles. 'Your aunt didn't live here did she, or did she?'

'No, she lived in Edgeworth,' replied Tilly. 'I just came this way from London in the hope of surprising my friend Frances, but try as I might, I can't get in touch with her.'

'So what're you gonna do?'

'I dunno, look for a B&B I suppose, try reaching her again in the morning and if I still can't get in touch, head on over to Bolton.'

'Why don't you stay here?' suggested Miles, a little too enthusiastically. 'I mean, if you want, if it's not too basic.'

'I wouldn't be under your feet would I; I wouldn't like to be in your way.'

Be careful,' whispered APONI. *'We don't want her staying here forever and mooching on the never-never.'*

'Never be under my feet Tilly, honest. Just hope, like I say, it's not too basic.'

'I've stayed in many places Miles much more basic than this love; I promise you.'

'Really?'

'Really.'

'Tee-pee's, rat infested log-cabins, bivouacs next to buffalo, abandoned flea ridden barns . . .

'Tee-pees!' proclaimed an alarmed APONI from a silent corner of Miles' mind. *'Really?'*

'Really?'

'I've had to travel a lot too with my job, spent a lot of time in the field.'

'Right, right, well. So yeah, stay here if you like.'

'I think I will Miles if you don't mind, I think I will,' replied Tilly with a congenial laugh which only served to further enamor Miles, 'Got any alcohol?'

∞

Tilly took Miles up on his suggestion that she take a nap while he rode his old butcher's bicycle with a basket on the front to go pick up some alcohol and food for the next couple of days and some other odds and sods, bits and bats. For the first time in a long time, he could see the appeal of Hebden and the canal, the fields that reached out as far as he could see, and for the first time in a very long time, he was aware that he didn't bathe as often as he perhaps ought to and that the 'authenticity' of his anarcho-punk appearance could well do with a slight compromise every now and again, particularly *now*, with the aid of a bit of soap and some washing powder. He fuckin' stank he told himself and decided that before he went anywhere near a shop, he was going back to the house that he (or rather, Periwinkle) was renting out, to dig out some clean, or at least cleaner clothes and to see if he could score a shower. The tenants there were long-time friends and wouldn't object to him helping himself to the bathroom by way of the spare key in a tin under a loose stone flag in the back yard should nobody be home. The challenge was, to make himself appear clean and presentable without making it obvious that he'd gone to any real effort, which in and of itself would be a task.

As he stood in the shower, he couldn't help but ponder over the cryptic nature of his earlier conversation with Pez on the phone. She'd seemed happy enough when he'd excitedly told her that Tilly was in town and in fact, on board *The Sunrise Warrior*, but Miles felt a little uneasy with the fact that Pez had also bumped into an old acquaintance from Bolton who may end up paying a visit to the boat, but wouldn't say who.

'It's a surprise,' said Periwinkle.

'A nice surprise?'

'I don't see why not.'

'Then just tell me.'

'I've told you Miles, it's a surprise.'

'Give me a clue then?'

'A clue?'

'Yes,' said Miles in the characteristic petulant tone that Periwinkle knew well and almost always capitulated to, 'Just a small one.'

'Okay,' replied Pez. 'Just a small one.'

'Go on then.'

'Well,' said Pez. 'What goes with nuts?'

'What?'

'That's your clue: what goes with nuts?'

'Nuts?' asked Miles. 'That's not a clue.'

'Think about it sweety, gotta go now. See you soon, ciao.'

'Seeds and nuts,' thought Miles to himself as he stuck his head under the shower and watched the filth circle the drain. 'Fruit and nuts, salt and nuts, nuts and bolts, nuts in May, nuts and berries: nuts and bolts? No. No,' repeated Miles to himself as he got out of the shower and dried himself off, 'No, not Bolts.'

Miles went down into the cellar where he and the occupants had agreed that he could keep some of belongings and he found a change of clothes. He'd washed his hair but made a point of not shaving as that would be an obvious sign to Tilly that he'd made an effort, he couldn't much grow a beard anyway, so he'd scrubbed what facial hair he did have with *Natural World Argan Oil Shampoo*: Vegan friendly & cruelty free.

Once showered and changed he rode his bike to the shop and stocked up with food and alcohol: bread, beer, beans, cheese and wine and a bottle of vodka. As he rode back to the boat along the towpath, he recalled happy times in years gone by of living not too far away from Tilly and them sitting up late at night drinking and smoking together, flirting almost. And, he remembered too as he furiously pedaled, he remembered her excusing herself on occasion to go spend the night with Frank, to lie in bed with Bolts; dirty Bolts the scrap metal collector from Atherton or Leigh or some such Hovis-speaking, pit-man, mill-talking shit-hole: 'Eee-eh, 'ey up,' Miles said to himself in scathing tones as he aimed the front wheel of his bike towards a frog that was hopping across the path: ''Ast bin't mill er wot me owd lad?'

Miles had been gone about an hour and a half and when he got back to the boat Tilly mouthed *hello* as she sat on deck with her legs dangling over the side as she spoke on the phone.

'You manage to get in touch with your friend?' asked Miles a few minutes later feeling jittery inside, hoping she hadn't, fearing she had.

'No,' she replied, to Miles' relief.

'No?' he said, in what he intended to sound like a sympathetic tone.

'You'll never guess who that was,' said Tilly holding up the phone, but he *could* guess, Miles knew for sure who *that* was.

'No idea,' he replied. 'Who was it?'

'It was Ray, sorry, Pez – Periwinkle.'

'Oh yeah?' said Miles, suddenly relieved. 'Is she on her way back here?'

'He is yeah, says he'll back in an hour or so.'

'Oh goody!'

'Okay,' then said Tilly, resigned now to the fact that like it or not, awkward or not, she'd be spending the evening socializing with her long-lost transitioning half-cousin Periwinkle. 'We can watch the telly together have a laugh, there's a documentary on about the Olympics.'

'Sport?' asked Miles. 'Really?'

'Well, if you don't want to, then . . .

'No, no,' replied Miles. 'It *is* the Olympics, so . . .

'Cool,' she interrupted. 'How much do I owe you for these beers and what not?'

'No, no, they're on me – my treat.'

∞

Tilly and Miles sat in the fore-well of the boat with the door open and the telly turned on with the sound muted as they each sipped from a can of lager and listened to the new Culture Shock album.

'What's it called this?' asked Tilly, tapping her foot to the anarcho-ska.

'*Mandemic*,' replied Miles.

'MAN-demic?'

'Yeah,' replied Miles without looking up from his task of rolling a three skinner: hash and tobacco.

'As in MAN representing humanity and DEMIC referring to pandemic?'

'I suppose,' he said looking up with a smile.

'Or,' she asked. 'MAN representing male?'

'I dunno, m'not sure.'

'Sounds a bit cheesy though don't you think Miles; you know, a bit middle-class tabloid and cheap: MANdemic, MANboobs or moobs, MANkles, MANbag and all that metrosexual office-worker with the neck tattoos and two braincells? What are they called, hipsters?'

'You don't like the title?' asked Miles. 'I think it's creative.'

'I wish they'd be less fashionable with their language and challenge the mainstream,' tutted Tilly with a laugh as she flicked back a lock of hair that had fallen over her shoulder, 'MANdemic! Are the lyrics on the inside of the CD cover?'

'It's online: maybe the lyrics are available online.'

Tilly had always liked Culture Shock, Citizen Fish and Subhumans: Dick Lucas the lead vocalist and primary lyricist had been prolific in his output over the past forty years but given her work schedule and what with bringing up the girls, she hadn't really had the time to keep up with the music that she grew up with. Still, it was great to see that the bands of her youth were still going strong and that they hadn't compromised the subject matter, their sound, or their ethics by signing to major labels. She looked up the lyrics to the song that was playing (*Mandemic*: the album title track) and hummed along before bursting out laughing.

'What's funny?' asked Miles, offering her the joint to light up.

'No thanks,' she said, 'I'll stick to the green; that stuff makes me dopey; this makes me think,' she continued, holding up the pipe.

'Seriously,' said Miles with exaggerated intrigue. 'What's funny?'

'These words to this song love, just tickled me.'

'Oh yeah, how come?'

'Says here, they say, "*The sea's gone brown and tastes like plastic bags and petrol, the extinction rate is up and it's not accidental; the land is overused or scorched or under water, humanity's a new disease there is no cure for*", that's what's funny Miles love.'

'Well yeah,' replied Miles, 'they've got a point there. I mean when they say the sea tastes like plastic bags they're obviously speaking metaphorically, and I would assume referring to the fact that there's a floating island of plastic in the middle of the Pacific Ocean that's apparently three times the size of France. That's not cool, and I think it's great that they're still singing about these kinds of issues and highlighting the evils of this world. They're right, humanity is a disease that there is no cure for, don't you agree Tilly? I thought you with you background in ecology would sympathize with that, surely?'

'The is no plastic island in the middle of the Pacific love, there're are satellite images which show the whole of the region and Hawaii is clearly visible. If Hawaii which is far smaller than France can be seen, how come an island of plastic waste three time the size of France can't be seen?'

'But I've seen photographs which clearly show large expanses of plastic waste in the sea, I've seen it Tilly.'

'I've seen those photographs too Miles. Here, let me look them up on my phone. Hang on a sec,' she said taking a minute scroll and load. 'Right, yeah, here they are. Are these the photos that you mean?'

'Yeah, there you go Tilly, plastic as far as the eye can see in the middle of the ocean.'

'I have to admit that is a lot of plastic and rubbish, but it's not as far as the eye can see and it's nowhere near three times the size of France, it's not even ocean litter as you might think of in the conventional sense.'

'So what is it?' asked Miles with a notable smirk that was intended to express his incredulity. 'Seriously, if it's not what you call conventional litter, what is it?'

'It's debris from the 2011 tsunami that hit Japan and other places in the region: it's not conventional litter love, really.'

'Really?'

'Yeah really.'

'And the petrol, what about the sea tasting like petrol like it says in the song?'

'D'you seriously think that the sea tastes like petrol Miles, I mean do you?'

'It might do in some places.'

'Like where?' asked Tilly.

'I dunno,' replied Miles. 'But somewhere.'

'Everywhere?' she pressed.

'Well no, not everywhere.'

'So, the lyrics are a bit of an exaggeration then wouldn't you say? 'Plus,' she added with a wink, 'sounds like it's been recording inside a biscuit tin.'

'I suppose, yeah. The production's not that good.'

'I think,' said Tilly, 'if they're going to write about these kinds of issues, they should be more specific. It would be better for the overall environmental cause if they identified the exact area where there was petrol in the ocean and point out the possible cause and offer some kind of solution, but to blame humanity for such a vague claim and say that we are a disease that there is no cure for is hyperbole and comical. To be honest, I'd have thought that after all these years of writing about social issues his work would have developed somewhat and become significantly more mature because to be honest Miles, the lyrics to that song are little other than an adolescent virtue signaling rant.'

'You really think so?' asked Miles.

'It's the exact same sentiment that you read about in the mainstream media or see on the BBC, ITV, Sky News or any other legacy outlet that oftentimes largely depends on exaggeration and misinformation to capture and retain the interest of the general population. National treasures like David Attenborough are making so-called documentaries of mass walrus death due to CO_2 and the public lap it up; it's a distraction from real and authentic environmental concerns.'

'Wait, what?' said Miles. 'What d'you mean David Attenborough is making that up; I've seen that documentary series, how?'

♭ - And the system tells such fucking lies,

why should I believe what they say is

true? asked APONI.

'He says that they haul themselves out of the sea not by choice but out of desperation, right? D'you remember, on the episode of *Our Planet* titled "Frozen Worlds" yeah?'

'Right, yeah. I've seen it. Me and Pez watched the whole series twice; it's one of the reasons we decided to get involved with Extinction Rebellion, or at least plan to, hope to soon, when everybody's been vaccinated and the pandemic is over with.'

'Really?' asked Tilly. 'When everybody's been vaccinated: d'you mean everybody or just everybody who's vulnerable?'

'Really,' replied Miles. 'We are in a multi-faceted crisis stemming from irresponsible human activity. The global temperature is increasing, the pandemic is worsening as the virus mutates and new strains begin to infect people, nationalism is on the rise and toxic masculinity stemming from white supremacy is rapidly proliferating.'

'And that's why you believe everybody should be vaccinated?'

'Absolutely,' replied Miles. '*Every*-**body**! Twice, and then boosted. And then like Israel's proposing, fourth: just get jabbed, it's not complicated.'

Part B: Political Love . . .

6.

'*Helloooow*,' Periwinkle almost screeched as she entered the fore-well of the boat and broke the silence between Miles and Tilly, 'I'm home!'

'Good weekend?' asked Miles.

'Wonderful,' replied Pez. 'Tilly, is that really you darling? Come here and give me a hug; how long has it been?'

'A while,' said Tilly as she stood and weakly embraced her half cousin before pecking the air by the side of each ear like celebrities do on the television when they pretend to know and like each another.

'A *real* while,' said Pez. 'Years, decades. How are you, where have you been, tell me all about it.'

'Well,' began Tilly. 'I just . . .

'But first,' interrupted Pez, 'let me tell you who *I* met on the bus over from Sheffield, you'll never guess. Did you guess Miles?'

'I think so,' said Miles as he pulled a disagreeable face and slowly shook his head before relighting the joint.

'Who?' asked Tilly.

'Go on Miles,' pressed Pez. 'Can you guess?'

'From what you said over the phone about what goes with nuts, I'm guessing Bolts?'

'Cooorect!'

'Who?' asked Tilly. 'Frank?'

Miles nodded and offered her the joint without saying anything but she once again declined before opening the bottle of Shiraz that had been sat on the table for

46

the past half-hour and poured herself a glass, as Pez announced she was taking a shower.

Miles nodded slightly in acknowledgement without looking up and Tilly inwardly smiled a little before sarcastically beginning, '*Sir David* said that global warming had melted the sea ice which the walruses usually used to haul out on, so out of despair, they had to haul out on land in unprecedented numbers. The claim was that there wasn't enough room so they had to climb up to 80 meters up a cliff but the fact is, they can't climb cliffs. What actually happened is that they waddled up a slope which unfortunately brought them to the top of a cliff. By the way, this was a colony of around 5,000 females and their cubs which seasonally engage in this kind of behavior. As more members of the colony hauled out onto the shore, others were forced to make their way along the slope and as they did, those at the top began to be forced over the cliff. It had nothing to do with any increase in CO_2 which was claimed led to the melting of ice for the walruses to haul out onto, and, it's claimed, Mr. Attenborough knew this to be the case. So, why is the public being misled by the narration of a man it has largely revered, respected and trusted for decades?'

'I don't know,' replied Miles. 'It's hard to believe that he would knowingly lie to the public and it's just as hard to believe that he wouldn't have known the truth, that is, if what you're saying *is* the truth.'

'A picture is worth a thousand words they say though right Miles love yeah?'

Miles shrugged and took a hit on his joint before asking, 'D'you mind if I have a glass of this wine?'

'Help yourself love.'

'But I bought it for you.'

'We can get another one later if we want one, right?'

Tilly handed him her phone to look at the image of the walrus colony that had hauled out and whose many members had been forced to inch their way up the slope to the top of the cliff over which hundreds had fell to their death.

'Where is that?' asked Miles.

'It's near a place called Ryrkaypiy on the Chukotka coast of northern Russia.'

'Yeah?'

'Yeah,' replied Tilly. 'And that many walruses attracted dozens of polar bears that inundated Ryrkaypiy, which some say should now be evacuated. A few years ago, the town would see around five bears per season, now they're reporting having seen over fifty.'

'But did they not go there because the ice was melting?' asked Miles.

'No, they went because there were easy pickings, thousands of walruses.'

'*Riiight*,' said Miles thoughtfully, though not fully convinced. 'The walruses.'

'Goo-goo-ga-joob,' sang Periwinkle, suddenly appearing in the fore-well from the aft end of the boat and the shower area with a wine glass in her hand. 'Or is it, "Coo-coo-ka-choo?" - Are we sharing?'

'Help yourself,' said Tilly picking up the bottle and pouring into Pez's glass. 'Cheers.'

'Really?' said Periwinkle in affected outrage after Miles had explained the discussion he and Tilly had just concluded about walruses, 'Sir David? Never! Really?'

'But,' said Miles. 'I'm not convinced that hauling themselves up onto the shore had nothing to do with an increase in CO2 and melting ice; if the ice melts it'll be more than walruses that are in trouble. This human disease will end itself, so perhaps Culture Shock are wrong Tilly when they say that humanity is a disease there is no cure for.'

'Maybe,' said Pez. 'Maybe the cure for the disease of humanity is more humanity to cancel itself out? Is that what you're saying Miles?'

'Well, it doesn't look like we're going to stop pumping poison into the atmosphere anytime soon really does it?'

'It doesn't,' replied Pez with a *tut* and a *tsk* before once again clinking wine glasses with Miles. 'Here's to the ironic end of humanity, at the very hands of humanity.'

'The problem is,' said Tilly, 'CO_2 isn't poison. An increase in CO_2 is good for the earth and we should be happy that there's been an increase and if the increase is due to human activity, we should be celebrating humanity as a savior rather than denigrating it as a disease for which there is no cure.'

'An increase in CO_2 is good thing?' asked Pez?

'It is yeah,' said Tilly. 'A very good thing.'

'Show her,' said Pez to Miles. 'Show her your tattoo.'

Reluctantly, Miles pushed up the sleeve of his sweatshirt on his left arm and tilted it so that Tilly could properly see the tattoo: An exact copy of the Hockey Stick graph that was the centerpiece of the Third Assessment Report that was published in 2001 by the United Nations Intergovernmental Panel on Climate Change (UN-IPCC) and which was authored by Michael Mann. Tilly recognized it straight away because it had become the primary justification for the claim that the earth's temperature was rising to catastrophic levels due to human activity. It was also the focal point for Al Gore's book and accompanying film, *An Inconvenient Truth*, for which in 2007 he and the IPCC were awarded the Nobel Peace Prize.

'Brilliant that don't you think Tilly sweetheart, yeah?' said Pez.

'Nice artwork,' she replied.

'But?' asked Miles, somehow knowing she had more to say. 'Go on,' he laughed good naturedly enough, 'don't hold back.'

'It's just,' began Tilly, pursing her lips to give the impression that she had to consider what she was about to say, 'it's just that the Hockey Stick Graph as it's widely referred to that you've got tattooed on your arm has been debunked and discredited several times, even by people who believe that more CO_2 is a bad thing and that it *is* humanity that is responsible for the irreversible and catastrophic changes that it's said are currently occurring.'

'But it's like the words in the song right Tilly,' said Miles as he sang, '*the land is overused or scorched or under water*. So, if more CO_2 is pumped into the atmosphere, then the temperature will rise and cause the ice to melt which will result in more land being under water.'

'That's right isn't it Tilly?' asked Pez. 'If the temperature rises, the ice will melt and coastal areas will be flooded?'

'Have you got any ice in the fridge?' she asked.

'There should be,' replied Pez who got up to check. 'D'you want some?'

Tilly got up and joined Pez in the kitchen: 'Good to see you again cous,' she laughed.

'You too.'

'You got a couple of pint glasses too?' said Tilly.

Pez pointed up to a cupboard and Tilly took out a couple of pint glasses, she then filled one half-full with ice and topped it up with water to about a quarter of a centimeter from the top. She then took the second glass and filled that too to a quarter of a centimeter from the top with just water before taking the two glasses and putting them on top of the television in the fore-well and explaining. 'Each glass is almost full but one contains an amount of ice while the other one doesn't, right?'

'Right,' said Pez

'Right,' repeated Miles. 'Sure.'

'Well let's see if the glass containing ice overflows once the ice has melted, okay?'

'Okay,' Miles slowly drawled, indicating his uncertainty. 'Okay, alright: I think.'

'Will it overflow?' asked Pez. 'We should move it away from the T.V. if it's going to overflow, will it overflow?'

Tilly stood up and moved the two glasses and put them on the shelf to the left of the entranceway after moving a set of keys and a newspaper: 'Here okay?' she asked.

'That's better replied Pez. Now what?'

'Now we just sit and carry-on chatting and see what happens,' said Tilly, 'once the ice melts.'

'Let me put a paper towel under this one with the ice,' fussed Pez to Tilly's amusement. 'Just in case of spillage.'

'You say,' said Miles to Tilly, 'you say that CO_2 is a good thing?'

'It is Miles, yes,' she replied taking a sip of Shiraz. 'M*mmm*, nice.'

'But that's not the consensus,' he replied. 'Most people agree that it's a pollutant, right?'

'What kind of primary school did you go to Miles?' she asked.

'How d'you mean?'

'Catholic, C of E, you know. What kind of primary school did you go to?'

'I went to a C of E school,' said Pez.

'Me too,' said Miles.

'And me,' said Tilly before asking. 'And did you meet each morning in an assembly and listen to the teachers talk about Jesus and then you all sang from a hymn sheet up at the front of a hall while some teacher played the piano or occasionally a guitar?'

'Mr. Johnson at our school couldn't play guitar for shit,' laughed Pez. 'But every time he got the chance, there he was up on the stage singing Kumbaya and strumming his "axe" for all he was worth.'

'And did most of the teachers in the room believe in Jesus; I mean, were they Christian?'

'I suppose,' said Miles. 'I suppose they were.'

'And the kids, were they Christians?'

'Yeah, but only by default.'

'But most people in that hall for years on end, day in and day out, believed in Jesus and the ten commandments and ideas like "turn the other cheek" and were segregated from Catholics and were told that their religion was the one and only true faith, right?'

'Right,' said Miles.

'Right,' said Pez.

'Right,' said Tilly. 'And did you believe in Jesus at the time?'

'I suppose I did,' replied Miles.

'And do you still believe in Jesus; d'you still consider yourself to be a practicing Christian?'

'Of course not.'

'But back then the majority of people believed that if you prayed to Jesus, he would hear you right and answer your prayers?'

'Right,' said Miles, knowing where this was going. 'I know where you're going with this.'

'So there was a consensus yeah?'

'Yeah.'

'Was that consensus correct in your opinion, you know, from where you stand today?'

'Not really,' replied Miles.

'No,' said Pez.

'Science doesn't rely on consensus Miles love, it depends on observable facts, and the fact is that the Hockey Stick Graph authored by Michael Mann represents his use of data from bristle-cone pines; even the suppliers of that data themselves warned against using it for temperature reconstruction. But politicians took hold of that graph and the surrounding narrative and promoted it, saying that the way to effectively combat this so-called deadly pollutant was to increase taxes.'

'I know,' said Miles. 'But if the government makes it more difficult for people to buy and use things like coal, oil and natural gas by raising taxes, their usage will decrease and there will be less CO_2 pumped into the atmosphere, which is a good thing right?'

'Right,' said Pez. 'That seems logical enough to me; I'm surprised it doesn't to you too Tilly.'

'And I'm surprised that a couple of middle-aged anarcho-peace-punks living on a narrowboat in Yorkshire are so easily taken in by politicians, then again I'm not.'

'You think we've been duped?' asked Pez good naturedly enough.

'Yeah,' smiled Miles, comically feigning injury. 'Do you? You do don't you?'

'Not only politicians,' she teased, 'but an AMERICAN politician like Al Gore no less. Enamored by his so-called earth-saving politics.'

'*Ohhh*, little lady,' said Pez. 'Aren't you the trouble maker?'

'Some things never change,' added Miles with guarded obsequiousness, before they each raised a glass: 'Cheers!'

7

Bolts was in his friend's back yard just finishing off putting the bike back together and bleeding the hydraulic brakes which, as usual, was a pain in the arse. His mate at been at work but had left the shed door open where the bike was stored along with the tools he'd needed to put it together so that he could ride it back over to Bolton. By the time he was finished it was late afternoon so he decided to contact Blister, or Periwinkle as he was now known, she: Pez.

'Yeah, come on over, we're just about to watch this program about the Olympics in Japan, should be right up your ally,' said Pez, trying to sound interested. 'D'you know where we are?'

'Not really.'

'Hang on a minute,' he told Bolts before turning to Tilly and Miles. 'It's Bolts, he's coming over but he doesn't know where we are.'

'Does he know where the off-license is, you know Miles, the one we passed this morning where you bought those Rizlas?'

Bolts said he knew where it was and Tilly said she'd take Miles' butcher's bike with the basket on the front and meet him there where she'd pick up another couple of bottles of wine and anything else they could think of that they might need. Miles wasn't too keen, but found solace in the fact that it wasn't he who had to pedal down the canal towpath to meet him. Once Tilly had left, Miles couldn't help but ask, 'Bolts? Why would you invite him of all people here Pez?'

'He's okay Bolts, got a fancy job in Shanghai or somewhere.'

'He's a thug.'

'He's not a thug; he's just not one for being pushed about. He's like me.'

Miles shrugged because Pez had a point. It's just that he wasn't nervous around Pez, whereas he was around Bolts, or at least had been thirty-five years earlier: 1986.

Tilly arrived at the off-license first and browsed the wine aisle looking for anything that might catch her eye, any two-for-one offers or three-for-two. She finally decided on three bottles of Australian Merlot, eight assorted bottles of micro-brewery beer, a couple of multipack bags of crisps and some tobacco for the lads, or, she then thought, the lad and lass. 'Periwinkle,' she said to herself. 'What the holy . . .

She was just loading the last of the bottles in the basket on the front of the butcher's bicycle when Bolts arrived, they exchanged a few words after a prolonged and increasingly tight hug and she waited outside while he went in and bought what he needed. 'Is it far,' he asked as they set off, 'this boat?'

'About fifteen minutes, not far.'

'So Blister, quite the er, transformation yeah?'

'You could say that,' she said. 'You could say that.'

'And how's Miles?'

'Miles is Miles,' she replied. 'No different, just a bit older.'

'Is he still a wet blanket?'

'Shush-up Bolts and behave yourself,' she said in a mock-reprimanding tone which told Bolts she was mildly flirting.

'A big girl's blouse?' he added.

'Behave yourself will you Bolts,' she giggled as she pedaled through the afternoon air, the stark and leafless trees against green grass and the rippling water of the Hebden canal as the odd boat chugged by: Rochdale.

'Fair enough,' he replied. 'As you wish.'

'And less of the Princess Buttercup routine if you don't mind,' she giddily snapped back, but he just winked before repeating, 'As you wish.'

∞

When they arrived at the narrowboat it was approaching dusk and somewhat and the light was now faded, though not enough to obscure the name of the barge: '*The Sunrise Warrior*?' asked Frank in a whisper.

'I'm saying nothing Bolts,' said Tilly before adding, 'Stop laughing and watch your manners.'

'So you made it Bolts,' said Pez. 'Have a seat mate.'

'Ta mate.'

'You wanna beer?'

'Does the pope shit in the woods?'

'Yorkshire's finest: Will a *Tod's Blonde* do you?'

'If Tod doesn't mind.'

Miles winced, glanced at Tilly who was opening a bottle of wine and flashed his eyebrows to illustrate his disapproval: Bolts noticed but said nothing.

'Do you want a glass?' asked Pez.

'No ta,' replied Bolts. 'I'm good thanks.'

'Oh, oh,' said Pez. 'Oh: the pint glasses and the water and the ice!'

'What's he on about?' asked Bolts, looking at Miles.

'She,' said Miles. 'Pez is a she.'

'Oh aye, really?'

'Really,' said Miles, softening his tone as he realized Bolts was holding his gaze. 'She identifies as female.'

'Was he born with a cock and balls?' asked Bolts.

'That's not really the point,' replied Miles breaking eye contact and reaching for the tin on the table before saying, 'D'you mind if I roll a joint Tilly?'

'Help yourself love.'

'If he were born with a cock and balls, and I know he were,' said Bolts, 'then he's a fella; I'm not being funny Miles lad, but bollocks to your wokery. Tinker in my yed at your peril.'

'I'm not tinkering, I'm just . . .

'You're attempting to convince me that my old mate over here is a woman; you're attempting to influence my perception of reality and nature itself with your daft ideas of feelings over facts, and I'm not having it Miles mate. Not from you, not from no cunt.'

'Well that all soon went downhill quickly didn't it?' said Pez. 'You've only been here two minutes Bolts.'

'You want me to fuck off or what?'

'Come on Bolts, nobody wants you to leave,' said Tilly. 'Enjoy your drink, you wanna smoke?'

'Okay,' he replied. 'So long as it's not any of yon brown hash shite: geet any green?'

Miles reached over to shake Bolts' hand: 'I'm sorry Frank; how you refer to Pez is between you and her.'

Pez patted Bolts' back and said, 'Frank can call me anything he wants, can't you mate?'

Tilly laughed and handed a loaded pipe of skunk to Bolts who took a couple of hits before offering it to Miles.

'I can't smoke green,' said Miles. 'It's too strong.'

'It's too strong, or your mind is too weak?' replied Bolts.

'I'll have some,' said Pez, who took a couple of tokes before handing it back to Tilly who reloaded the bowl and handed it back to Bolts who took another hit before offering it to Miles.

'Go on then,' he said. 'If everybody's having a go.'

'But look at the pint glasses,' then said Pez as Miles was taking a second toke on the pipe. 'The water levels are the same now that the ice has melted and there's no watermark on the paper-towel I put under the glass that had ice in it.

'So what?' said Miles. 'What does that prove?'

'Displacement,' said Tilly. 'The melted ice that is now water has replaced the ice and the level has not changed. If the Arctic were to melt, there would be no increase in sea level as the doom-mongers say there will be.'

'But that's not what the scientists say,' said Miles, 'and Al Gore, Extinction Rebellion.'

'What?' said Pez. 'Ninety-seven percent of all scientists?'

'And,' added Tilly, 'as far as the Antarctic goes, it's much the same. In 2017, there were reports of melting ice shelves surrounding the Antarctic Peninsula, but like the Arctic, they are floating and therefore displace water in warmer times when melting occurs. There was a lot of media hype when part of the Larsen C Ice Shelf broke way in the middle July of '17 and both those with a genuine concern for environmental issues and opportunists alike used the event to claim that humans were to blame.'

'But you've got to admit,' replied Miles, 'you have to acknowledge the fact Gaia would be in better condition if we humans had never come into the world. Right?'

'Gaia, as in Mother Earth?'

'Yeah,' said Miles. 'Mother Earth.'

'You think that if humans, as you say, had never come into the world, it would be a better place: really?'

'Really,' he replied. 'Much better.'

'You respect the earth and all that comes from it then, nature-wise I mean yeah?'

'Of course. The earth would much better without people, or at least white people and their appetite for control. Don't you think?' he concluded with an air of affected incredulity. 'Don't you?'

'I don't believe that humans came into this world in the same way as I think you do Miles; I don't believe we came into the world at all.'

'What d'you mean Tilly? Every childbirth is celebrated by acknowledging the arrival of the baby into this world.'

'You seem to believe that humans come into this world, whereas I think that people come from the earth. The earth sprouts trees, bees, flowers, pigs and people Miles love,' laughed Tilly. 'We don't come to this world or into it, we come from the planet that you believe is Gaia or Mother Earth.'

'But look at the damage we do?'

'Look at the damage that the wind does or the rain, the sun or tornadoes.'

'That's just nature going about its business though Tilly.'

'And you believe that humanity isn't a part of nature and you'd rather view us as a species with original sin?'

'You're making it sound pseudo-religious, whereas it's a spiritual outlook.'

'Viewing humanity as some sort of plague on the planet is spiritual?'

'Yeah, well at least I think so,' said Miles before nervously asking: 'You don't?'

'No Miles love,' she replied. 'I don't. And, any increase in sea level comes not from floating ice masses such as the Arctic or the Antarctic, but from glaciers that have formed on land and then melted and glaciers form and melt all the time.'

'I'm not sure,' said Miles suddenly beginning to feel a little uncomfortable as he began to feel the weed paranoia begin to rise and his need to contact APONI.

∞

After Miles had lit some sage and smudged the place to shun away any dark spirits that may have entered with Bolts, he returned to the table in the fore-well and sat glassy-eyed staring at the television, silently chanting with APONI, as Tilly and Pez talked on about ice and sea levels as they squinted at a graph on Tilly's phone. Bolts was in the kitchen chopping an onion for the spaghetti sauce that he was making. Periwinkle then decided to go and lie down for an hour on one of the two beds in the aft after announcing that she was tired from the week's direct action training sessions. As he was preparing the food, Bolts could hear Miles and Tilly talking through the partition that separated the fore-well from the kitchen area and inwardly laughed to himself at the thought of cultivating a spiritual outlook based on the belief that humanity was a plague upon the earth. 'Never get into her knickers with a line like that mate,' he then said to himself as he reached for the green and red peppers. 'Not in a month of Sundays.'

'No,' he heard Tilly reply, 'not at all,' before she asked Bolts. 'You watching this documentary on the Olympics?'

'Has it started?'

'Just starting.'

'Not really bothered to be honest. D'you want any spaghetti?'

'Go on, I'll have a bit,' she said.

'You Miles?'

'Same thanks, just a bit.'

'Reet y'are.'

'It's just that we've done so much damage,' said Miles as he fully muted the volume on the television which had been on low. 'Say there is no plastic garbage patch: what's it called?'

'The Great Pacific Garbage Patch.'

'But still, even if it's like you say and it doesn't exist, you still get sea birds feeding bits of plastic to their young which then leaches out toxins and kills thousands of birds which I can only think is going to lead to a growing number of birds becoming extinct. It's not right Tilly, it's just not right.'

Bolts had chopped the onion, green and red peppers, garlic and was now preparing the broccoli which he'd boil for a short time: he liked broccoli in his pasta sauce and he was looking forward to Tilly's response because he's read the book by Patrick Moore, one of the founding members of Greenpeace back in 1971 when Bolts was eight years old and Leigh had won the Challenge Cup final against Leeds, *Fake Invisible Catastrophes and Threats of Doom*. From reading the book and watching interviews with Dr. Moore, Bolts had learned that Sir David Attenborough was ostensibly not the great British national treasure that he'd previously imagined the fella to be, as it appeared that the avuncular naturalist and BBC shaman of all things rustic, was guilty of playing slight-of-slur. Once the broccoli was partially boiled, he put it aside and added some olive oil to a hefty frying pan that he's found in one of the cupboards and once again cocked his ear.

'There's a good reason why adult sea birds feed their young small pieces of plastic,' said Tilly.

'A good reason,' exclaimed Miles, 'for feeding plastic to their young?'

'Absolutely. More wine?'

'Thanks,' replied Miles. 'Not bad this stuff is it?'

'It's not no,' said Tilly before continuing. 'You've been watching David Attenborough again haven't you love?'

'Got the DVD boxset and me and Pez have binge-watched it twice over and it's one of the reasons why she's so enthusiastic about getting involved with Extinction Rebellion,' repeated Miles before asking, 'Anyhow, where is she?'

'He's gone for lie down,' said an unseen Bolts from the kitchen area. 'Said he were knackered from his week of training.'

'I'm beginning to worry about her,' said Miles in a lowered voice to Tilly. 'I think she might have long-covid because she's always tired.'

'He wrote a book,' replied Tilly. 'You know, Sir David.'

'He's written a few hasn't he?'

'He wrote one called *The Life of Birds*.'

'Yeah well,' Miles said. 'He knows his stuff.'

'You think?'

'You don't?' asked Miles.

'To be honest,' said Tilly. 'I hope he doesn't.'

'You hope he doesn't?'

'Birds don't have teeth so they can't chew their food to break it down before it enters the digestion process,' began Tilly, 'which is why they have a second stomach, known as a gizzard. The gizzard is a muscular stomach which grinds the food down before in enters the regular stomach, the one like ours, which aids digestion by way of stomach acids and what not. Anyway, birds often swallow small objects into their gizzard to help the grinding process. They use small stones or pumice, seeds, wood, the beaks of squid and among other things, pieces of plastic. Those birds are not feeding their young plastic for the purpose of nutrition, they're doing it for the sake of aiding digestion and since David Attenborough has written a book titled *The Life of Birds*, you would think that he would know that sea birds often resort to feeding small pieces of plastic to their young so that the muscles in their gizzard can use it or them to grind their food down before it enters the regular stomach and the digestive process continues.'

'So what do you mean?' asked Miles. 'I hope he doesn't.'

'I mean that I hope he doesn't know his stuff and that he's a complete fake when it comes to narrating documentaries or commenting on anything regarding the environment because if he does know that birds have a gizzard and need to ingest small hard items to aid the digestive process, then he's lying for a living while all the while presenting this harmless and endearing amiable image to the nation, something that he's been doing for decades.'

'Spaghetti or pasta shells?' asked Bolts, suddenly appearing from the kitchen area. 'Any preferences?'

'If he's not a fake,' continued Tilly, for the moment ignoring Bolts, 'and he does know his stuff, then he's a propagandist and the BBC license fee payers are being conned and their money is being used against them. Not only that Miles love, but they're being threatened with prosecution and fines if they refuse to pay the fee which is used to mislead the public and shape public opinion, government policy and proposals for legislation. Just a sec Bolts please. And, if he genuinely doesn't know his stuff, the public is paying to listen to nonsense. Either way, something's not right, you see my point?'

'Speaking of gizzards,' said Miles. 'Shells for me Bolts: Tilly?'

'Oh, sorry Frank. Either for me.'

'Shells it is,' he replied before disappearing back into the kitchen area where the water was beginning to come to the boil.

'It's hard to believe that they could be so blatantly misleading on purpose,' replied Miles. 'That's sincerely evil.'

'Been at it for years,' quipped Bolts, reappearing from the kitchen. 'Should be ready to eat in ten minutes if *you're* ready.'

'Can we wait awhile and eat later?' asked Tilly raising her glass. 'I'd rather drink for now.'

'No prob, later's fine.'

'Been at it for years?' queried Miles, surprised at the domesticated affable nature he saw in Bolts, yet still unable to shun the image of busy tin-snips from his mind's eye.

'Well, what I mean is,' said Bolts. 'Is this the last of this bottle?'

'It is yeah,' replied Tilly. 'I'll open another.'

'Ta Tilly. What I mean Miles, is when we were tiny kids, it was fear from the threat of almighty god above who was watching our every move and keeping a score card that we'd have to account for come the start of the afterlife at the Pearly Gates. Then when we were teenagers, it was the threat and the fear of nuclear annihilation, complete with images of women and children running down the street with their skin hanging off their bodies and tales of radiation sickness and a nuclear winter that would last for fuck knows how long. Then it was the Big Freeze when everything was going to be frozen over and folk would be skating on the Thames; then it was the bloody hole in ozone layer; then global warming; then climate change; then manmade catastrophic climate collapse which has led to a pandemic and the lockdown of countries across the globe, death, devastation, newly created emergency vaccines and disintegration of business, culture and civil liberties and of course,' wound down Bolts, before concluding with a sarcastic flourish and a wink which slightly unnerved Miles, 'the plan to build back better and create a new world order. Ta-da.'

'Shiraz or Merlot?' asked Tilly.

'Either,' said Bolts

'Same,' replied Miles before continuing. 'Either. But, David Attenborough?'

'Plastic is harmless,' replied Tilly. 'Plastic litter may be an eyesore but it doesn't leach toxins. All litter is an eyesore. I mean, take a look outside here in Hebden where you live, it's beautiful. What's the problem? Where's the problem?'

'There are problems,' said Miles.

'Where?' asked Bolts.

'Well, not here, I suppose. But, there are problems.'

'But where?' asked Tilly.

'I'm not sure,' replied Miles. 'Everywhere I suppose.'

'A lot of places I've seen are way worse than Hebden,' said Frank a few minutes later, noticing that the documentary had started. Parts of China are filthy beyond belief and heavily polluted.'

'There's pollution round here,' replied Miles. 'Some people leave litter lying around and sometimes idiot dog walkers don't pick up the mess their dogs leave; we have to act.'

'A bit of wind-blown litter and one or two dollops of dog-do doesn't really compare with the pollution in other countries though, does it?'

'Depends where you're talking about; where are you talking about?' asked Miles.

'Where are you talking about?' said Bolts.

'New York's polluted,' said Miles. 'Australia has problems.'

'The top ten most polluted countries,' began Tilly, scrolling at her phone, 'are, starting with the most polluted first: Bangladesh, Pakistan, Mongolia, Afghanistan, India, Indonesia, Bahrain, Nepal, Uzbekistan, and at number ten, Iraq.'

'But what kind of pollution is it?' asked Miles. 'And what's causing it?'

'Says here,' said Tilly. 'Says that Pakistan's minister for climate change blames India but the citizens of Pakistan blame the Pakistani government for not doing enough to monitor or combat the crisis. Each country is slightly different in regards to the source of pollution but as far as Pakistan goes, it's a mixture of an increase in the number of cars, loss of trees . . .

'Maybe they need more CO_2,' said Bolts, popping his head around the partition. 'Trees like CO_2, it's more or less all they eat.'

. . . smoke from brick kilns,' continued Tilly, 'steel mills, and the burning of garbage.'

'But that pales in comparison to Australia's problem and the bleaching of the Great Barrier Reef though right?'

'Really?' asked Tilly.

'Jokes aside though Bolts,' replied Miles, 'CO_2 is the primary pollutant the world over and is the cause of the death - or should I say - the near death of the Great Barrier Reef, which is serious right because it's the largest living organism on the planet. That's really serious.'

'The Great Barrier Reef has recovered from the bleaching event of 2016 and anyway,' said Tilly, 'CO_2 didn't cause the coral to bleach and lose its color and to be what was widely claimed at the time, almost totally dead.'

'*Mm*,' said Miles thoughtfully. 'Really?'

'Really. The majority of reefs are a relationship between an animal, the coral, and a plant, the plankton. Coral contains up to hundreds of thousands of polyps that absorb the plankton which is then protected from predatory grazers and which use water and CO_2 to produces sugars, some of which feed the polyp. On occasion, when the surrounding ocean temperature for some reason increases or decreases, the coral ejects the plankton and so then appears bleached, but the fact is, coral polyps are transparent. It is the plankton which give the reefs their color. In fact, there are occasions when the plankton is ejected that the coral also spawns which means the reef is essentially reproducing as opposed to, as many in the media have been claiming, dying.'

'Seriously?' asked Miles with, once again, an air of incredulity. 'Really?'

'Seriously,' replied Tilly.

'So why has there been so much alarm over the issue of the bleaching of the Great Barrier Reef? How come all these scientists are claiming that there's a problem and something needs to be done and done as soon as possible? I don't get it.'

'You don't get it because you're too nice Miles,' said Tilly as she reached over and briefly touched his hand. 'Like many people.'

'Many people?'

'Many people simply can't allow themselves to step away from the tragic story that's been planted in their head. It's a story in which they, along with the beneficent scientists and the media, businesses and governments which support the story, play the part of some sort of gladiator against evil. But the thing is, CO_2 is not the great evil it's made out to be because in fact it's food for plants which in turn is food for animals and us humans. It isn't carbon dioxide which is evil, it's the scientists that are clamoring after the millions of dollars and pounds or whatever in research grants that are morally compromised. They are evil.'

'I can't believe that scientists, well-educated and professional people would or even could for that matter, purposely mislead so many people for their own financial gain.'

'It's not just financial gain,' said Tilly. 'There's the desire for professional advancement and recognition, an increase in status from peers, friends and family. You can't believe that scientists could or would mislead people because, like many people, you're too nice, and because of that, you assume that most people, particularly professional people, are nice too.'

'I can't honestly say that I really feel like a nice person.'

'You feel guilty?'

'In a way.'

'Why?'

'I'm not sure, maybe for not doing enough.'

'A lot of ordinary people are afraid of what they believe is catastrophic manmade climate change and feel guilty for not being able to do anything about it. Fear and guilt, they go together hand in glove. The western world is full of individuals of all ages who are riddled with anxiety and somehow blame themselves and their fellow human beings. It's like Bolts alluded to earlier about when we were kids and we were taught about original sin and made to feel somehow guilty for what Adam and Eve had done.'

'I recall back in school,' said Bolts who was stood by the partition comically, though unknowingly so, blowing at a wooden spoon that contained pasta sauce. 'I recall back in school getting caned across the arse for not singing hymns during morning assembly and later being warned at break time by a teacher not to retaliate when this kid kicked at my legs as we were going down the stairs to the playground.'

Miles was suddenly a little surprised at Bolts' comment, the fact that he'd relayed a tale about being a kid and apparently bullied by somebody kicking at his legs because the tin-snip gossip just didn't allow for *any* kind of vulnerability to be associated with Bolts.

'I didn't like that,' Bolts had continued. 'I didn't like the fact that I wasn't allowed to stick up for myself but the institution, the school and well-educated, professional adults, they were allowed to cane me (a kid) across the backside in retaliation for breaking their rules by not singing their hymns in praise of the god that said I was guilty for what Adam and Eve did, which as far as I'm concerned was fuck all other than to eat an apple and then get dressed. The original sin was to eat an apple and put some clobber on and yet these days, Christians get all in a tizzy when folk take their clothes off. According to the Christian faith, shouldn't getting naked be akin to going back to a time before original sin and therefore being closer to god? D'you like garlic?'

'I'm good with garlic,' replied Tilly.

'Me too,' said Miles with a wry smile across the table at his friend as Bolts returned to his cooking.

'He's harmless,' she silently mouthed across the table. 'You shouldn't worry.'

Miles nodded in acknowledgement without looking up at her, a second later suddenly alarmed due to Bolts - who was stood pointing at the muted television with his wooden spoon - having yelled, 'Britain's got a gold!'

'Turn it up,' said Tilly. 'What event?'

'Not sure,' replied Bolts. 'I'm just surprised.'

'Black lives matter?' asked Miles sarcastically, taking a slightly inebriated light swipe at Bolts as he noted the black face on the screen.

'Of course they do; all lives matter. Thing is, the organization is a sham.'

'I don't agree,' said Miles.

'Fair enough: fine.'

'Back to the polar bears,' replied Miles, not really wanting to wrangle with Bolts. 'That's an issue: climate change due to manmade mistakes is an issue. I mean, we can't sit back and witness the extinction of polar bears, can we?'

'Polar bears wouldn't exist if it wasn't for climate change,' said Tilly: PhD. 'Polar bears migrated north across the Bering Land Bridge from America some ten to twenty thousand years ago when the area was colder and covered in more ice. Then, when it got warmer and the bridge of ice melted, the brown bears in the arctic circle evolved to have a white coat for the purpose of camouflage.'

'They could still mate though yeah?' said Bolts. 'I mean, if they were ever in the same proximity?'

'Theoretically,' she replied. 'They could yeah.'

'So what changed the climate back then to cause the melting of the ice bridge that allowed bears, and I presume other animals, to be able to migrate?' asked Miles.

'The sun,' said Tilly, 'is the most likely culprit when it comes to geological time and the naturally oscillating characteristics of climate change, the advent of an ice-age and then its recession and what are known as interglacial periods.'

'You just don't sound too concerned,' replied Miles with a wry smile that suggested he thought she was mistaken.

'I'm not,' she said. 'I can see that you are, and many other people I know for that matter, but why?'

'Because,' replied Miles, 'it's like they say; we're in unprecedented times.'

'Like who says?' she said.

'Everybody: the news outlets, the politicians, the professors and teachers, musicians and artist and actors, all of my friends, everybody I know.'

'And how are we in unprecedented times.'

'Because we're facing a global problem on several fronts: the collapse of the climate, this pandemic, and the rise of white supremacy.'

'Oh yeah?' asked Tilly, returning the wry smile.

'Yeah, we're in unprecedented times and humanity is facing an existential crisis that will most likely see the extinction of thousands of species and the eventual death of our planet. Doesn't that bother you?'

8

'I'm a scientist Miles love,' said Tilly, 'and the words "most likely" aren't part of my vocabulary when it comes to this subject, particularly in relation to any kind of basis for policy proposal. It's the language of Extinction Rebellion and its half-baked ideology.'

'Half-baked?' asked Miles. 'How so?'

'Well, what exactly do they stand for, what precisely do they want?'

'They want three things,' Miles replied before correcting himself. 'WE want three things.'

'And what are they? And where's Bolts?'

'I'm back here,' said Bolts. 'Has Britain scored anymore gold medals?'

'We turned it off love, lost interest. You don't mind do you?'

'Na, never followed it really but if it's on, I can enjoy it.'

'The first thing they want,' Miles continued, 'is for the government to tell the truth.'

'About what?' asked Bolts.

'About the truth: Our first DEMAND is that . . .

'Demand?' Bolts asked, suddenly appearing at the partition, to which Miles replied, 'Yes, DEMAND.'

'Go on. Your first demand is what?'

'Our first DEMAND is that the government tell us the truth . . .

'Don't let us down,' Bolts suddenly began singing, though Miles had no idea why.

'The government,' he continued, 'should tell us the truth about the irrefutable fact that there is a looming climate catastrophe and ecological emergency . . .

'What's your worth to a pile of earth, your just another man,' Bolts then interjected, once again singing.

'. . . and work with other institutions to work for change.'

'Oh yeah?' Bolts asked. 'Anything else.'

'Our second DEMAND is that the government must reduce greenhouse gas emissions to net zero by 2025 to halt the loss of biodiversity by acting NOW.'

'And what's net zero?'

'What's net zero?' Miles replied.

'Yeah, what's net zero?'

Miles just looked at him with complete bewilderment ironed across his face at him having the gall to even consider asking such a question.

'Net zero,' he replied, 'is not an easy concept to explain.'

'Net zero,' interjected Tilly, 'is the balance between the amount of CO_2 that is put into the atmosphere and the amount which is removed.'

'That's it,' Miles said. 'Net zero emissions is the balance between the amount of CO_2 that's removed from the atmosphere and the amount that is put into the atmosphere.'

'Oh yeah?' said Bolts. 'Any other demands?'

'Our third and final DEMAND is that government must go beyond politics.'

'How so?' he asked. Bolts asks a lot of annoying questions thought Miles; he really is, as the Americans would say, an asshole.

'The government,' replied Miles. 'The government must create a Citizens' Assembly and then be led by its decisions on climate and ecological justice.'

'Why does the government need to create a Citizens' Assembly? I mean, why don't the citizens create a Citizens' Assembly?' asked Bolts.

'Because,' Miles replied, 'if citizens create it, then the government won't really pay any attention to it.'

'Well, if they won't pay attention to it once it's created, what makes you think that the government will pay enough attention in the first place to create a Citizens' Assembly? And anyway, what the fuck is a Citizens' Assembly in the first place when it's at home?'

Miles had no idea how Bolts could be so apparently ignorant on an issue, THE ISSUE, of the 21st Century. He couldn't abide such seemingly willful ignorance about the elimination of biodiversity, the guaranteed destruction of the natural world, the planet: the patriarchal and white supremacist degradation of the universe. And neither could he understand why it was that Tilly wasn't speaking up on the issue since she was the one with a PhD in Ecology; maybe she's was just being sarcastic with her silence. Yeah, she's probably is just being ironic with her silence in order to prove a point, her point, Miles' point.

'It says here,' said Miles, 'on the XR website, "The Citizens' Assembly will be run by non-governmental organizations under independent oversight", which sounds reasonable enough yeah?'

'But what is it?' asked Tilly.

'Wait,' said Bolts. 'You and others that support Extinction Rebellion want the government to set up a non-governmental organization?'

'Absolutely,' replied Miles. 'It has to be a non-governmental organization because the government can't be trusted to earnestly and effectively run it.'

'Then what makes you think that the government can be trusted to set up a non-governmental organization when you believe that it can't be trusted to run one?' queried Tilly.

'That's what I were thinking,' said Bolts. 'If XR members or sympathizers or whatever set up a Citizens' Assembly - whatever it is, probably some kind of committee of some sort - then they could then present it to the government for them to

72

acknowledge its validity and get on board with the overall cause and begin to take measures to address your concerns yeah Miles?'

'The government won't recognize our Citizens' Assembly if we set it up, they have to do it.'

'But what is it?' asked Tilly again. 'I don't get it.'

'It says on their website,' said Miles, scrolling at his phone, "The Citizens' Assembly on Climate and Ecological Justice will bring together ordinary people to investigate, discuss and make recommendations on how to respond to the climate emergency. Similar to jury service, members will be randomly selected from across the country. The process will be designed to ensure that the Assembly reflects the whole country in terms of characteristics such as gender, age, ethnicity, education level and geography. Assembly members will hear balanced information from experts and those most affected by the emergency. Members will speak openly and honestly in small groups with the aid of professional facilitators. Together they will work through their differences and draft and vote on recommendations".'

'Balanced information from experts?' asked Tilly.

'That's what it says,' replied Miles before adding, 'Sounds logical enough to me.'

'And who,' enquired Bolts with a sarcastic smile, 'who exactly will decide who these experts are? To be honest, I don't think any scientist who may have any opinion that's strays from the doomsday narrative would ever be allowed anywhere near an Extinction Rebellion Citizens' Assembly.'

'That's a bit pessimistic Bolts don't you think, a bit . . .

'Would you want anybody involved who held the belief that the current levels of CO_2 are not a problem?'

'That,' scoffed Miles, 'wouldn't really be conducive to our overall cause, at least in my opinion.'

'Well there you go then . . .

'There I go where then?' asked Miles.

'There you go carrying water for the crony capitalists and the groveling to the government by supporting Extinction Rebellion and Insulate Britain which are little other than pseudo-grass roots organizations that are, whether they know it or not, nothing more than distractions from real issues.'

'Like what?'

'Like idiotic lockdowns, jabs before jobs, restricted travel . . .

'Lockdowns are a good thing,' replied Miles. 'As are vaccinations and restrictions on travel, and who people can and can't meet with and where and when . . .

Bolts smiled and hummed: 'M-m-m-m-m-m-m-m-m/m . . . ♪

'What *is* that tune?' asked Pez who'd been stood between the fore-well and the galley. 'I'm sure I know that song.'

Bolts just smiled, flashed his eyebrows, and sucked his teeth.

Miles was aware that what he supported and advocated regarding the Extinction Rebellion manifesto was in essence, illogical. If he was honest with himself, it was hypocritical and misleading because Bolts had a point which was that any XR Citizens' Assembly wouldn't tolerate input from any scientist or for that matter anybody whom didn't agree with the premise that greenhouse gases, primarily CO_2, needed to be reduced by 2025 in order to preserve biodiversity. However, Miles also knew that as an activist, he had to prioritize the goal over things like logic and the avoidance of hypocrisy.

'You think?' asked Bolts. 'You think lockdowns are good and net zero is a necessity?'

'We have to preserve biodiversity Bolts, and we have to act now - or rather the government needs to act now - by first telling the truth and then committing to net zero emissions by 2025 and the creation of a Citizens' Assembly.'

'And those are the three demands of Extinction Rebellion and people like yourself who support what it stands for?'

'We stand for truth,' replied Miles. 'Here, let me clarify by reading from their website: "We are facing an unprecedented global emergency. Life on Earth is in crisis: scientists agree we have entered a period of abrupt climate breakdown, and we are in the midst of a mass extinction of our own making".'

'But,' said Tilly, 'that's not actually true is it?'

'What's not true?'

'Well,' she replied. 'I guess the main thing that strikes me as being untrue is the claim that we need to reduce CO_2 in order to preserve biodiversity.'

'And how's that untrue?'

'Like I said earlier love, CO_2 is food for all plant life, which in turn provides nutrients for animals and humans alike. WE could use more CO_2, not less.'

'But it's increasing the global temperature.'

'In some places, humans are responsible for the increase in temperature, but it is only in some places.'

'Like where?' asked Miles.

'Like UHI's.'

'UHI's?'

'Urban Heat Islands,' she clarified. 'An urban or metropolitan area that is significantly warmer than its surrounding rural area due to human activity.'

A few minutes there came a buzzing sound from the aft of the boat and Miles and Bolts shared a smile, Tilly had stepped out to use her phone and her footsteps could be heard aloft.

'What's she doing?' said Miles.

'I dunno what he's up to Miles mate, but it sounds suspicious to me. Does *she* own a Rampant Rabbit?'

Miles blurted wine into his mask at the image of Periwinkle busy with a Rampant Rabbit and got up to rinse out his mouth and locate a clean mask: Two. Bolts reached for the remote, turned on the television, flipped through the channels once and turned it off again just as Miles retook his seat across the table from where Bolts was now sat in the fore-well. The buzzing continued as Miles and Bolts sat in silence, now and again smirking at each other.

'Why don't you wear a mask?' Miles finally asked.

'I'm not concerned about catching the virus,' replied Bolts before adding, 'D'you mind if I stick a tune on? I'd like to cover-up that noise back there.'

'S'okay,' said Miles, who then looked up a playlist and pressed PLAY.

'Why don't you wear a mask?' repeated Miles.

'Like I say, I'm not worried about catching the virus.'

'You could pass it on.'

'I don't have covid.'

'You could be asymptomatic.'

'Then if I have no symptoms, I wouldn't be able to pass it on would I? You had covid?'

'I have yeah,' said Miles. 'You?'

'Not that I know of. You been jabbed?'

'Three.'

'You've had three vaccinations, had covid and recovered from it and so therefore now have the antibodies and you wear two masks, yet it seems that you would feel more comfortable if I put on a mask right?'

'Right.'

'Why?' asked Bolts. 'How come.'

'I'd just feel safer.'

'What like, your masks don't work? Your antibodies and vaccinations are ineffective?'

'Like I say,' said Miles, 'I'd just feel safer.'

'Well, if your masks are ineffective, what makes you think that any mask that I wear will be effective?'

'I can't make you wear a mask Bolts, we both know that. But, I would feel overall safer if you did wear one.'

'I've not got one.'

'I can give you one.'

'Okay,' said Bolts. 'Let's have a look what you've got on offer. I'm promising nowt mate because them things you're wearing look like they've been cut from a pair of owd black jeans and then daubed in paint to fashion an anarchy symbol.'

'They're better than nothing,' replied Miles, returning to his seat after having fished out a couple of black masks. 'Here you go.'

'Looks a bit ragged this does mate, when was the last time it was washed. Who last wore it?'

'I keep a couple to one side,' replied Miles. 'For guests and visitors.'

'I'll pass,' said Bolts.

'Why?' whined Miles.

'Where're the anarchy signs? If your masks have anarchy symbols why can't my masks have anarchy signs?'

'I'm in the middle of making some new ones.'

'But don't you think that people should have the freedom to decide for themselves whether or not they wear a mask, you know, anarchy symbols aside?'

'Hang on,' said Miles. 'I might have another mask here with an anarchy sign stenciled on it; won't be a sec.'

Bolts inwardly smiled to himself at what he saw as the dire yet ultimately dangerous pettiness of it all, the lack of awareness, the blind acceptance. But it wasn't just so-called ordinary people like Miles. He'd recently seen some footage of Justin Trudeau, the Prime Minister of Canada, giving a somewhat impassioned speech that included the idea that Canadians would not be mandated to be vaccinated and they would always have the choice whether or not they get jabbed. However, Trudeau went on to say, those who chose not to get vaccinated against covid-19 should not expect to be able to get on a plane or a train and sit beside vaccinated people and put them at risk. Surely, thought Frank, the vaccinated were not at risk, or much less at risk, from contracting the disease, simply due to the fact that they had been jabbed. If they were, then that was surely proof positive that the vaccines were ineffective. And anyway, would it matter if the person they contracted the disease from had not been jabbed? Bolts had another mate who had told him that they had had a bad dose of covid and then after recovering had chosen to get jabbed, twice. Surely concluded Bolts, there was no need to get vaccinated if they had had the disease because they would have the antibodies to fight off any further contact with the virus. The whole situation he reckoned to himself, was now less about any real medical issue backed up by science and had morphed into an us-against-them scenario and occupied the territory of ideology and political affiliation in the ongoing culture war.

Miles on the other hand felt that Bolts was simply being selfish because the majority of scientists, as far as he could tell, supported and advocated the wearing of masks, mass vaccination and other cautionary measures such as social distancing, restricted contact with other people, self-isolation, quarantines and lockdowns. But it wasn't just the scientists, it was the health-care workers and doctors, virologists, mayors, M.P.'s, politicians of all stripes, big business and big-tech. What right had Bolts got to think that he somehow knew better than these highly educated, experienced and esteemed leaders of their fields? None. Stephen Fry, one of Britain's national treasures was on board with Extinction Rebellion and had made a video that was up on YouTube. If Stephen Fry, one of the most well-educated intellectuals in the nation, indisputably one of the most talented men in the U.K. could see the validly of the cause of XR, why couldn't Bolts? Obviously, Bolts was a Neanderthal compared with Stephen Fry; Bolts was an idiot, larping as an everyman when he didn't need to because most working-class idiots were idiots, there was no need to larp. Bolts was a slave to idiocy: why wouldn't he just wear a couple of masks when he hadn't been jabbed, not even once. Why not wear just one? There was only one thing more important thought Miles to himself, as he opened and closed drawers and cupboards in search of a mask that had stenciled on it an anarchy sign, and that was the challenge of addressing the inevitable collapse of the climate, the extinction of humanity and thousands of other innocent species and the eventual premature rapid decay of planet earth. Bolts he concluded, as a tear or two began to well in either eye, was the epitome of cock-sure selfish sods that were steering the world to undisputable wrack and ruin because after all surmised Miles, the coronavirus was a direct consequence of climate change and the degradation of the planet by humans, by man, or rather men – white men.

'I can't find another mask with an anarchy sign on it,' said Miles, having dried his eyes, as he returned from the near aft to the fore-well. 'You don't want to wear that one?'

'Miles mate,' replied Bolts. 'It's just a piece of cloth cut from an old pair of jeans with shoe laces attached to loop round your ears and it's not been washed in a while so no, I don't want to wear it.'

'Okay,' shrugged Miles with an exaggerated sigh. 'Suit yourself.'

'And besides, it's dirty to wear masks day in and day out for months on end.'

'Why is it dirty Bolts? I mean, I wash a batch every two or three days and use clean one each, when I can. They're not dirty; why are they dirty?'

'Because CO_2 is something that humans breath out: we exhale CO_2 and inhale oxygen. Trees and plants do the opposite. The CO_2 that we exhale is bodily waste, which although might well be beneficial to trees and plants, is waste matter to people. You wouldn't voluntarily sniff your own farts all day long would you or drink your own piss. Like piss, farts, shit and snot, CO_2 is bodily waste and to wear a mask day in and day our limits the body's ability to fully get rid of it in the way that nature intended.'

Part C: Reality Attack . . .

9.

Tilly entered the fore-well from the outside of the boat just as Miles re-entered from the kitchen area where he'd been fishing around for a bottle opener: 'Any luck?' he asked.

'Yeah, she might be able to give me a lift over to Bolton tomorrow. Said she'd get back to me later.'

'That's great,' lied Miles. 'Brilliant.'

'Covid aside for the time being,' said Bolts. 'I'm interested in Extinction Rebellion and its demands; or rather, the claims that have been made over the past couple of decades or so because like many people, I have an interest in this.'

'Yeah?'

'Yeah: I took a course toward my degree over thirty years ago titled, *Man, the Economy and the Environment.* I've had an ongoing interest ever since.'

'Everybody ought to have an interest,' replied Miles.

'I think most people do,' said Tilly. 'It's just that there is no universal agreement on exactly what the problems are and how to fix them, if at all that's possible.'

'That,' replied Miles. 'Is exactly why we need a Citizens' Assembly.'

There was a sudden silence that hung in the air as the buzzing in the aft came to a conclusion and Tilly, Miles and Bolts pulled on cigarettes, swished wine around in a glass or stared at their reflection in the now blank television screen.

'You heard of the notion of War Profiteering Miles mate?' Bolts eventually asked. The Military Industrial Complex and the idea of certain people making money from war, the suffering of others and the death of thousands or tens of thousands or more?'

'Of course I have,' replied Miles.

'And you Tilly?

'Sure, a lot of punk bands and journalists and all manner of sources have remarked over the years about the Military Industrial Complex and War Profiteering. Why?'

'Well I was wondering, what d'you think makes certain people look beyond the welfare, safety and lives of other people for the sake of making more money than they already have, especially when they have more than most? What is it that prompts politicians and people in business to collude in a manner that would appear immoral to most, not all, but most ordinary folk?'

'The bottom line,' shrugged Tilly, taking a sip of her Merlot. 'Money.'

'Money,' agreed Miles. 'Money, greed, a lack of morals and capitalism.'

'You don't think that this kind of collusion took or takes place in communist, fascist or any other economic or political system?' asked Tilly.

'Yeah, I suppose you're right,' replied Miles. 'Though the Americans and their brand of capitalism is notorious for this kind of exploitative collusion between politics and big business which leads to death, destruction and the abandonment of all moral or ethical considerations.'

'Agreed,' said Bolts. 'And Tony Blair and Britain followed in lock-step when Bush the Second claimed that Saddam Hussain had weapons of mass destruction that could reach us or our allies in forty-five minutes yeah?'

''Yeah,' said Miles, suddenly feeling the discomforting and unwelcome encroachment of certitude. 'Something like that.'

'I must admit,' acknowledged Tilly. 'It is America that is most widely known, along with its number one ally Britain, for propagating this business model, this military industrial complex and War Profiteering.'

Bolts let the conversation settle awhile, as though allowing a campfire to die-down prior to throwing on more highly flammable material. Tilly mused to herself, quietly contented that the three of them had come to an agreement, while Miles felt strangely elated that he had gotten Bolts to seemingly admit that George Bush had lied and misled Tony Blair about WMDs.

'So,' said Bolts. 'D'you find it easy to believe Miles that people like George Bush and others would lie to millions of people in order to manipulate them into supporting their cause; the notion that Iraq was in possession of WMDs and that Britain and its bedfellows were in imminent danger?'

'I do find it easy to believe that George Bush would manipulate the truth for the sake of lining his own pockets and yes I do believe that he put the lives of Iraqis and Afghanis in a category which placed little value on them when it came to War Profiteering: people like that care nothing for human life, they just lie, cheat and thieve to make money for themselves and their ilk while others perish.'

"*They lie, we die . . .* ♪

'Then why,' asked Tilly of Miles, as she glanced at Bolts, 'Then why do you find it implausible that a man like Al Gore and his ilk couldn't also be lying and cheating in order to line *their* pockets.'

'Exactly,' said Bolts. 'You're readily willing to acknowledge that there is such a thing as War Profiteering, though somehow you're reluctant to entertain the thought that there is such a thing as Climate Profiteering: Why is that?'

'Yeah Miles love,' said Tilly with a wink. 'Why is that?'

'What are trying to suggest Tilly, that Al Gore and all the scientists and Extinction Rebellion care little about the earth and the climate and the average person? Climate Profiteering?'

'Do War Profiteering arseholes lie and kill in order to turn a profit?' asked Bolts.

'Sure they do,' replied Miles. 'Of course.'

'And,' continued Bolts, 'do, what I'm calling Climate Profiteering arseholes, lie and kill in order to turn a profit?'

'I don't believe there are such people that you can label as Climate Profiteers.'

'It's a thought experiment Miles,' suggested Tilly. 'Run with it.'

'Then no,' said Miles, 'they don't. At worst they lie, but they don't kill.'

'So,' asked Bolts, 'if you can bring yourself to believe that some people (War Profiteers) lie and kill to make money, why is it that you can't bring yourself to believe that some other people (Climate Profiteers) simply lie and mislead to make money? Which is worse, to lie and to kill or to lie and mislead?'

'I'll have to think about that,' replied Miles. 'I'll give it some thought: I need more details.'

'Wait,' said Tilly. You seriously need to think about which is the worse: to lie and kill for money or to lie and mislead for money? Seriously?'

'What I need to think about,' said Miles, 'is exactly how much the government is involved in this because it appears to me that it's not involved at all, which is the problem. Remember, our first demand is that it tells the truth; the second is that it acts now by committing to net zero by 2025; and the third is that it gets beyond politics and set up a Citizens' Assembly. Now!'

'This is a global issue right Miles love?'

'Of course, and America is the biggest offender.'

'The Citizens' Assembly that you want; will it be national or international – global?'

Miles wasn't sure whether the call was for each nation to have its own Citizens' Assembly which would then be distilled into a global version of itself, or whether each national assembly would remain autonomous, he just knew that the governments of the world, particularly the western countries need to act now. Western Europe needed to act, and that included Britain, but the biggest offender and most egregious of carbon emitters was of course the U.S. of fuckin' A-man.

'Fair-weather rebels this XR lot if you ask me,' said Bolts with a laugh. 'Seem to come out in late August and early September. You don't actually see much of them in February or March when it's cold and pissing it down do you?'

Miles said nothing but inwardly felt that both Bolts and Tilly were now somehow ridiculing him because he couldn't answer their questions, didn't have all the information. He might not have a fancy job in Shanghai or wherever like Bolts or a

PhD like Tilly, but at least he cared, at least he could cry for the degradation of the planet and weep for the loss of biodiversity. Suddenly he felt as though his personal space had been invaded and he was no longer safe from the in-joke he felt sure the two were now sharing behind his back, in front of his face. He wasn't sure that these two were now welcome he thought, before chastising himself: "Shut-up you fuckin' idiot, it's Tilly you skunk-stoned idiot, she'll always be welcome. Bolts though? I just wish he'd fuck off back to Shanghai or Tokyo or Leigh or wherever he would so choose, just well away from here in Hebden and myself and Tilly and Periwinkle".

'You said earlier Miles mate,' said Bolts scrolling at his phone, 'you know, about this Citizens' Assembly concept and the third of Extinction Rebellion's demands, that, "The process will be designed to ensure that the Assembly reflects the whole country in terms of characteristics such as gender, age, ethnicity, education level and geography. Assembly members will hear balanced information from experts and those most affected by the emergency. Members will speak openly and honestly in small groups with the aid of professional facilitators. Together they will work through their differences and draft and vote on recommendations". That's what you read to us earlier right yeah?'

'Yeah,' said Miles. 'That's it, why?'

'I'm just wondering,' replied Bolts, as Tilly got up from the table with a smile and headed into the kitchen area. 'Will the Assembly or committee or whatever it is be comprised of representatives from these groups of people in the same percentages as they are present in the general population? If so, how can we really know how many gay, lesbian or bisexual people there are in the country and seriously, what has sexuality got to do with the weather, the climate? And, there are some people from certain religious groups who believe that women shouldn't be involved in such decision making and who are also very much opposed to homosexuality as it goes against their deeply held spiritual beliefs. How on earth are all these conflicting interests going to be reconciled is my question. The demand for a national Citizens' Assembly to be set up by the government, which the government should then be subservient to is problematic enough, then given the diversity of the make-up of it is just guaranteeing conflict. If there is a plan or any intent to create an international version, the diversity of identities and opinions is going to multiply exponentially and there'll be even more conflict. Any such Assembly, whether national or international, is little other than wishful thinking and would take well beyond the 2025 deadline demand for carbon net zero to set up and let run its course through the decision-making process. It's a dead-loss before it's even started mate.'

'We have to do something,' replied Miles. 'Anything. Doing nothing is not an option.'

'But the demands are flawed from the start,' pressed Bolts. 'The first demand for the government to tell the truth is flawed because the whole idea of catastrophic manmade climate change is multi-faceted and there is no consensus on many of the individual issues. There have been many claims that the science is in and such like, but in actuality, those claims are more to do with either mainstream politics or grass-roots activism than the employment of the scientific method.'

'Well . . . ,' began Miles, but he was cut short as Tilly and Periwinkle entered the fore-well from the kitchen area. 'Well what the heck have . . . ?

Bolts applauded and Tilly rubbed the palm of her hand across the newly shaven head: 'You've shaved your head Pez?' asked Miles in disbelief.

Gone was the effeminate and camp intonation and the hair, and gone too were the pink canvas Converse shoes and the tight skirt and the tights and in their stead a pair of camouflaged shorts and a black t-shirt with the band name *Discharge* and the words, **Fight Back**.

'I'm done Miles mate, and no more *Pez* or *Peri*-fuckin-*winkle* or *Bliss* for fuck's sake. My name is Raymond Burns and I'd prefer to be called Ray or Blister; preferably the latter.'

'No more transitioning?' asked Miles.

'No more transitioning,' replied Blister.

'I'll drink to that,' said Tilly.

'Me too,' agreed Bolts.

'Okay,' said a confused, and somewhat disappointed Miles. 'I think. I think I'll open a new bottle of wine.'

10

'Any chance I can get any decent weed around here?' asked Bolts when the celebrating had died down and everybody had rapidly downed two half glasses of red wine apiece. 'Either tonight or tomorrow morning before I head off over to Bolton.'

'I know where we can get some,' replied Blister. 'If we go now. It's just a couple of miles down the cut here, we can take the bikes if you're not too pissed.

Miles felt suddenly elated that the **new** Blister and the **old** Bolts had decided to leave for an hour or two, hopefully longer. Talking to Tilly alone was a charm and one tarnished in the company of Bolts, so the sooner he went the better. Bolts and Blister could catch up and natter about the old days during the early eighties before any of them had moved over to Nottingham. That was a time before Miles really knew Blister, who at that time was socially closer to the then scrap metal collecting Bolts, who on occasion, slept with Tilly: A thought which Miles' mind scurried to exterminate.

'Reminds me of when you lived on Park Road Miles love,' remarked Tilly once Blister and Bolts had departed, 'and I used to drop by and chat, sometimes stay the night on your couch.'

'Long time ago Tilly, but I remember those times well. What did we talk about all night long?'

'Life, the past, the then present, our futures. We were young and uncertain, full of unwarranted confidence: confused without knowing it I suppose.'

'Yeah,' said Miles, 'too true: young and uncertain; no more though. The past is done, the future is questionable and it's now in the present that we need to act, before it's too late.'

'Too late for what love?'

'We're at a tipping point Tilly, we've got little time left to save the earth. Alexandria Ocasio Cortez said twelve years and that was a couple of years ago and Greta Thunberg said pretty much the same around the same time.'

'And,' replied Tilly. 'In 2009, that's twelve years ago, Prince Charles said we had only eight years left; in the eighties we were told by the United Nations that "entire nations could be wiped off the face of the earth" due to rising sea water if we didn't act by the year 2000. Also, in 2009 at the Copenhagen UN climate summit, Al Gore said we needed to reach a climate agreement immediately: "We have to do it this year," he demanded, "Not next year, this year".

'Yeah?' asked Miles, feigning surprise with a fabricated smile, hamming-up the interest.

'In January of the same year,' continued Tilly, 'James Hansen from NASA said that Obama had "four years to save the earth" and in October 2009, Gordon Brown reckoned we had only fifty days to prevent a climate "catastrophe". In March of 2009, Elizabeth May of the Canadian Green Party claimed "we have hours" to prevent climate disaster.'

'So, they got it wrong.'

'They did that Miles love, they did that. And, what's more, NASA gets 1.5 billion dollars a year from the federal government for climate research. Over the past twenty years, politicians and activists of any number of nationalities and political stripes have been making predictions that have turned out to be way off the mark but have served to mobilize people across the world, particularly in the Anglosphere and other developed countries, into berating anybody and everybody who doesn't fall in line with their, "the end is nigh" narrative, and the absolute need to do something NOW, though anything they ever suggest, only ever turns out to be far-fetched and impractical. Your national Citizens' Assembly Miles love will never work in the timeframe that is being demanded which is net zero before 2025 because there are too many conflicting parties being invited to the table, the big pink table that does nothing but serve as a theatrical prop for a middle-class hissy-fit.'

'Why don't you say what you think Tilly?' said Miles, though in a tone which suggested that he admired her insight and tenacity. 'You might have a point.'

'I took a course, well a workshop really I suppose, on the history of climate activism and although the scare stories have been going on for a long time, they really began to enter the public consciousness about fifty years ago with the global cooling scare. It was "Plant a Tree in '73" and the threat of the world collapsing within a couple of decades, then in 1987 it changed to "global warming" and the hole in the ozone layer because we were using fridges and what not. Then in 1988 the UN-IPCC was formed and three years later it published its first assessment report which since then has been updated every five or so years and is now referred to as the "climate bible". It's just part of our culture Miles love, this doomsday crap: global cooling, population bomb, nuclear winter, ozone layer depletion, global warming, climate change, catastrophic climate change, imminent catastrophic climate change, imminent manmade catastrophic climate collapse. You can bet the Chinese are pissing themselves at us right now; either that or the CCP is utterly envious of the degree to which western governments can effectively employ propaganda. It's bullshit Miles.'

'But if it is bullshit, who's behind it and what's the intent? I can't believe that all those people out on the streets in London have been fooled Tilly. There are some really intelligent people out there fighting to save the planet, wanting what's best for the next generation and the one after that and the one after that and so on. I don't get it, it's confusing. If I'm honest, I cry on a regular basis for the state of the earth, most genuine people do.'

'Crying has become a fashion Miles. Ever since the election of Donald Trump in 2016 when people were applauded by their peers for expressing their personal disdain through tears in public; it's a bit mad if you ask me. No offense love, but *I* don't get *that*!'

'Like I say, I did cry at that,' said Miles, 'if I'm honest. That and Brexit.'

'You cried because Britons voted to leave the E.U. and opted for a smaller government? I thought you were an anarcho-punk love?'

'What d'you mean *though*?' asked Miles. 'Of course I am.'

'I thought anarcho-punks were in favor of smaller, more local governments, if any at all, rather than that of a vast superstate far away, unelected and unaccountable.'

'I just thought that to leave would be to show patriotism which is often linked to nationalism which in turn is seen to be racist.'

'And is it?' asked Tilly.

'Is it what?'

'Is nationalism the same as racism?'

'I think so. Yeah, I think so.'

'So you think Fidel Castro was a racist?'

'He was a communist,' replied Miles.

'He was a Marxist-Leninist and a Cuban nationalist Miles, and he prided himself on being so.'

'I suppose so: Maybe you're right.'

Miles was enjoying bending to Tilly's will at times as he felt it made him come across as reasonable and measured, emotionally mature and intellectually solvent. Inwardly however, he was aiming to buy time and as they continued to speak, hoped to retrieve one or two cogent points which would serve to rebut her premise and impress her; her premise that stated that meeting the 2025 target for net zero carbon emissions would never work because there were too many parties with conflicting ideas being invited to the table. He said he saw her point, but he didn't, or rather didn't want to and therefore didn't.

'I see your point,' he said. 'I see what you're saying but I can't understand why people would claim that we only have a limited amount of time left, whether or not they are mistaken, when they don't mean it.'

'It doesn't matter if they mean it does it Miles? I mean, it doesn't matter how earnest they are if they are wrong and all that they are doing is hedging their bets in order to be able to look good and secure the approval of their peers.'

'Ah?' asked Miles. 'How so? Surely, any mistake, even if purposely misleading *can* under the circumstances be qualified as a silk-stocking lie, a mistruth lined with good intent?'

'How so? Well, you ever heard of Connie Hedegaard?'

'No,' said Miles. 'Can't say the name rings a bell. Should it?'

'She is the former European Climate Commissioner and in 2013 she's was reported as claiming, *eerrr* . . .

'Claiming what?'

'Hang on,' said Tilly, scrolling at her phone. 'I have it saved somewhere. Ah, here it is. She was reported as claiming, "regardless of whether or not scientists are wrong on global warming, the European Union is pursuing the correct energy policies even if they lead to higher prices", which essentially means, even if the science is wrong, the global policy she was advocating was correct.'

'And where's that from?'

'The *Telegraph*.'

'Well, that's the problem then isn't it right?'

'What?'

'*The Telegraph* is right-wing and can't be trusted.'

'You only trust left-wing sources?' asked Tilly?

'Of course, don't you?' laughed Miles.

'You only trust left-wing sources and yet you call yourself an anarcho-punk?'

'Anarchy is rebellion against the status quo and the Tories are right-wing and in power and are therefore the status quo that needs rebelling against: nobody likes a Tory. At least nobody I know. You've not turned Tory have you Tilly?'

'You're a left-wing anarchist, an anarcho-communist?'

'I'd say that's the closest definition that I feel comfortable with, yes.'

'And which anarcho-communist publications do you rely on to get trustworthy news and accurate scientific commentary on say, the issue of climate change?'

'I don't,' replied Miles without even the slightest inflection of sarcasm as he got up to make his way to the toilet. 'I usually just watch the *BBC* and *Sky News* or read *The Guardian*.'

Tilly sat there alone at the table while Miles was taking care of his personal business, her elbows on the table-top and her face buried in the palms of her hand-kerchiefed palms as she made every attempt to stifle the erupting laughter. Uncompromising and dogmatic are two terms often associated with the word ideologue and Miles, thought Tilly, had without doubt become an ideologue. Maybe he'd always been an ideologue, their past interactions had been too long ago for her to accurately recall but he hadn't changed much and she felt that many she knew from decades ago had never moved on and in fact prided themselves on never having changed, or rather, never having added nuance to their ephebic political perspectives. They appeared fossilized, stuck in a past that was now vague at best to Tilly: sepia, motheaten and passe.

'I was reading *The Guardian* the other day,' said a now settled Tilly once Miles had returned and was retaking his seat at the table. 'An article by Nick Cohen in which he says that climate change deniers are just as bad as those who justified the slave trade.'

'That's right yeah,' replied Miles. 'That's right, I read that. He has a column in *The Observer*.'

'He begins by saying that the right-wing climate deniers of a decade or so ago are now remembered as dangerous fools, if they're remembered at all.'

'Too right,' said Miles. 'I can't recall who they were but anybody who denies that we have a problem is probably far-right and beneath being remembered. The world would be better without such insensitive idiots Tilly, they're as bad as anti-vaxxers, scum.'

'Well anyhow,' replied Tilly as she topped up each of their glasses with what was left of the Merlot. 'The thing is, the second paragraph opens with the claim that, "The **billions of dollars** spent by the fossil fuel industry on propaganda and its acceptance by know-nothing elements on the right caused incalculable damage", and there's a link, which it's assumed confirms the dollar-amount claim but . . .

'Yeah?'

'But when you go to the link, which is another *Guardian* article, and then follow the links to the data, the content is blocked.'

'Yeah, but,' said Miles, 'everybody knows that the climate-deniers are funded by the fossil fuel industry, so it doesn't really matter whether or not he has any proof, does it?'

'Doesn't it?'

'I don't think it does, does it?'

'Of course it does. You can't just say, *the claim that these people are making is not sound because they are being paid off by special interests and I claim to have the proof but cannot provide it but it doesn't matter because those who are making the claim are paid off by special interests and everybody knows that.* That's not a logical and coherent argument is it Miles love?'

'It doesn't need to be logical and coherent; it just needs to be true.

'But is it true?'

'Of course.'

'Prove it.'

'Proof isn't required when everybody knows that it's true: everybody knows that Tilly.'

'But what if I can offer you a different perspective Miles, one that would suggest that global warming promoters receive far more money than these so-called skeptics.'

'Why would you do that?' asked Miles. 'Wouldn't that be counterproductive to our cause?'

'In the interest of genuine scientific inquiry, objective truth, and to avoid being manipulated by propaganda. That why I'd do that love.'

'Truth,' declared Miles, 'is subjective: Objective truth is fascism and therefore invalid.'

'Objective truth is fascism?'

'Given our current predicament, yes. Absolutely.'

'Objective truth, as in mathematics, physics and chemistry, is fascism?'

'Those things are from the western world, so of course they are examples of fascism.'

'And what about dentistry?' asked Tilly. 'You can't deny that the science behind modern dentistry which has over the past three or so centuries saved innumerable lives all across the globe.'

'Same,' said Miles without knowing why.

'But modern, western dentistry, has saved the lives of many over time. Before modern dentistry people were dying left, right and center before they were thirty.'

'The world is overpopulated so saving lives is eco-fascism,' smirked Miles.

'Seriously?' she asked.

'Seriously,' he shrugged. 'Modern medicine is an example of the white man's eco-fascism. The truth is what we make it.'

The sun was now set in the far distance, a number of dogs could be heard barking at some unknown irritant, though no one knew what: a passing cyclist, a cat on a wall, hunger in the belly, the scent of a bitch on heat or the sound of a possible intruder? The mid-distance aerial song of the skylark was now retired, though nearby a wood pigeon cooed and grackle grittily cawed as Bolts and Blister slowly pedaled along the canal bank in search of a narrowboat named *Thistle & Thyme*.

'How far is it?' asked Bolts. 'This boat we're looking for.'

'It's just up here a bit; see that bridge . . .

'Yeah.'

'A couple of minutes past that if that's where he still is.'

'Who's *he*?'

'S'name's Badger, known him for years. He bought weed off me back in the nineties and early noughties when we both lived in Nottingham. Sound lad, bit damaged like but he's harmless.'

'Damaged?'

'E's and whizz: too much acid and not enough sleep; bad food, soap dodger. Probably a bit of a smack head on the snide.'

'Decent weed though yeah?'

'Yeah, his brother grows it on some remote farm or some place in Lincoln.'

Just as Blister had explained, the *Thistle & Thyme* was moored to two stakes driven deep into the bank just two minutes or so past the bridge. However, Badger wasn't home and the dreadlocked, middle-aged and grime-lined white lady whom answered the door had politely but insistently told them that he'd gone to pick-up and he'd be back within the hour, though they couldn't wait on-board as she was busy. They agreed to wait by the bridge and come back later, leaving her to her quarrelling on the phone.

'How will we know when he's back?' asked Bolts.

'His bike will be on deck by the door. He's got one of these old butcher's bikes with a basket on the front, they've been popular around here for some time now. He's painted his bright orange with green stripes and it looks hideous but he says that's the point. Says it's so noticeable and ugly that nobody will nick it and he's probably right. If we go up top on the bridge here, we'll most likely be able to see him arriving home when he gets there.'

'Fair enough,' said Bolts as they left their bikes and hiked up-top before pulling out two cans of *Guinness*. 'Want one?'

'Cheers mate, ta. Say, were Miles giving you some ear-bashing earlier about wearing a mask or was I hearing things?'

'Said he'd feel more comfortable mate if I wore a mask and when I asked him if he'd had covid and/or been jabbed, he told me that he *had* had covid and that he'd been double jabbed and boosted. *And* he was wearing two masks. When I asked him why he wanted me to wear a mask when he was wearing two after having recovered from the virus and therefore presumably having the antibodies and the natural immunity for his body to defend itself from any future attack and having been jabbed *thrice*, he said he'd just feel more comfortable if I wore a mask.'

'Did you?'

'Did I fuck.'

'Don't blame you: mithers me to fuck he does – yak, yak, fuckin' moan mate, I'm telling you.'

'*Ahh*,' said Bolts. 'He means no harm, just a bit nesh like - born mard.'

'True enough,' agreed Blister. 'But he's been a good friend to me over the years.'

'I don't doubt it mate, not one bit.'

Bolts, although hungry for answers, bit his tongue and benched any questions he had about the sudden change in Blister's appearance and demeaner since bumping into him earlier in the day in Sheffield. He was well aware that he shouldn't take the piss but couldn't help but have a go when he'd noticed the lad was wearing a bra. For the past thirty years Bolts had been around the more sensitive middle-class types in academic environments and he'd frequently been sidelined and shunned for not toeing the line when it came to being politically correct, for not being subservient enough to the deified vocabulary of the so-called progressive left. He'd thought it one of the fundamentals of punk to avoid being p.c. and remembered one of his favorite bands had included a track entitled NPC (Not Politically Correct) on their second album which was released in 1988. To be disenfranchised by middle-class colleagues from other countries or other parts of the U.K. on other continents meant little to Bolts but in recent years it was obvious from comments and attitudes on social media that the rot had set in and even the most hardcore of his old mates seemed to have taken to warbling woke do-good-ery in an attempt to let the world know that they too were well p.c. and therefore beyond reproach. Blister had looked like a right tit earlier in the day but nobody would ever say anything to him out of the fear of being ostracized and lambasted, insulted or even kicked and punched. It's like some perverted version of the Emperor's New Clothes, thought Bolts to himself as he looked off into the distance along the canal towards the *Thistle & Thyme*, wherein every little tosspot is suddenly sovereign and can't see the wood for the trees.

'You're not going to ask?' asked Blister.

'Nope.'

11

'The truth is what we make it?' asked Tilly.

'That's what most progressive minded people believe,' replied Miles.

'And do you?'

'Sure,' he shrugged. 'Why not?'

'So everybody's truth is equally as valid as each other's yeah?'

'Yeah.'

'Then Miles love, how would you really expect the required diverse group of individuals in an Extinction Rebellion Peoples' Assembly to come to any expeditious decision with respect to reaching net zero by 2025? If everybody has their own subjective truth because there is no such thing a valid objective truth, how will the assembly ever reach a decision?'

Miles simply smirked and shrugged and Tilly, unused to such a candid admission, decided to push back a little. In her academic circles, such a frank admission to the belief that everybody's truth is equally as valid as each other's would be ignored because that's not how science works. However, she was now beginning to fully realize that her good friend here was not an academic in any sense of the word and that he was first and foremost an activist. She had lost several friends in the past due to being on the other side of the fence so to speak, for being a researcher rather than a self-avowed radical. It slowly began to dawn on Tilly that her friendship with Miles had over the years dissipated and although it was now in the process of regenerating, it might at any moment and in the blink of an eye, evaporate. It had happened before over similar *and* dissimilar issues.

'The members of the assembly would come to make a decision by patiently listening to each other with respect and by acting with dignity,' replied Miles. 'And, with the aid of a trained coordinator, a consensus on how to achieve net zero by 2025 would be reached.'

Tilly was nodding to illustrate that she was listening and following along. She even consciously pursed her lips some in an effort to indicate that she was mulling over what Miles had said as she once again scrolled at her phone.

'You believe that the United Nations Intergovernmental Panel on Climate Change is a legitimate organization Miles love?'

'Of course,' he replied. 'It, along with Al Gore, won the Nobel Peace Prize in 2007. Its reports are considered the gold standard of its field.'

'Well then,' said Tilly, 'you might find this interesting.'

'What is it?' asked Miles taking a sip of Merlot, his left leg crossed over his right knee, his left foot beginning to dance a little. 'Where's it from?'

'It's from an article back in 2010 that quotes a UN-IPCC official who had worked as co-chair of Working Group III of the 2007 report and also as a lead author and . . .'

'Oh yeah?'

'Yeah. He said, and I'm quoting now. He said, "One has to free oneself from the illusion that international climate policy is environmental policy. This has almost nothing to do with environmental policy anymore, with problems such as deforestation or the ozone hole".'

'Does he say what it *is* about?'

'Interestingly enough Miles love, he does.'

'Go on.'

'He says, "One must say clearly that we redistribute de facto the worlds' wealth by climate policy. Obviously, the owners of coal and oil will not be enthusiastic about this".'

'And who said that?' asked Miles.

'Ottmar Edenhofer, co-chair of the UN-IPCC's Working Group III. He was also a lead author on the UN-IPCC's Fourth Assessment Report which was released in 2007.'

'Well, if he works for the United Nations Intergovernmental Panel on Climate Change, he must know his stuff. I'm sure that such a prestigious organization recruits only the most qualified scientists.'

'He's not a scientist Miles love, he's an economist. A German economist.'

'Oh yeah?'

'And influenced by guess whom?'

'No idea,' said Miles.

'Go on, have a guess.'

'Can I have a clue?' asked Miles.

'*Do you really believe in Thatcher*?' sang Tilly.

'Who?' asked Miles. 'Maggie?'

'No, silly.'

'Who then?'

'*Do you really believe in Marx?*

'So, this guy,' says Miles. 'What's his name, this German economist who was on the UN-IPCC panel, he reckons environmental policy is no longer about the environment and more to do with the redistribution of wealth is influenced by Marx, who was himself in favor of the redistribution of wealth?'

'That's what it looks like love, yeah. Ottmar Edenhofer appears to be saying that climate policy is not about environmental policy and is about the redistribution of wealth.'

'Marxism by the back door?' asked Miles.

'Apparently,' replied Tilly.

'But what's wrong with that? Marxism as an economic theory is sound right? The rich should be taxed more and the wealth should be more fairly and equally distributed to ensure equity, an equal outcome right Tilly?'

'That's not what Crass thought.'

'What did they think?'

'*Do you*,' Tilly began to sing, '*really believe in Marx?*

Miles just sat, foot dancing and face frowning, giving the impression that he knew not what she was talking about before finally saying: 'I'm not sure where you're going with this.'

'*Marx sucks*,' Tilly continued singing.

Miles, not wanting to concede that he hadn't recognized the anarcho-punk song that Tilly was referencing, smiled to himself a little without looking up at her and reached for the bottle of Merlot which was now more or less finished.

'I'll open another,' said Tilly. 'Shiraz okay with you?'

∞

'We should have brought a bottle of wine with us,' said Blister twenty or so minutes later as he scrunched up the empty *Guinness* can and handed it to Bolts to put in his backpack. 'Got any more cans?'

'Na,' just fetched the two. 'Think he'll be wom yet, what's his face?'

'Badger.'

'Aye Badger,' said Bolts. 'Reckon he'll be back yet?'

'Best if we hang back a bit really,' replied Blister. 'Sapphire's a bit temperamental.'

'Sapphire?'

'His misses; her who were having a barney on't phone.'

'Is that her real name, Sapphire?'

'Fuck knows: probably not.'

'So go on then,' Bolts eventually ventured. 'Tell us what got into you to ever imagine you could become a girl and . . .

'A woman!' insisted Blister, before amending his tone by way of self-deprecating mimicry, 'Not a girl.' The pair were tickled now; wine, beer & weed giggles – belly laughter.

'Go on then,' said Bolts. 'Spit it out.'

'I suppose that I was inspired by Edweena Banger back in 2016, somewhere between Brexit in June and Trump in November. Trans-issues had been quite the topic in the activists' circles for some time and one thing led to another.'

'How so?'

'Well, you've noticed how Miles likes to wear these flowery Laura Ashley dresses over his black jeans and . . .

'Yeah.'

. . . and anyhow, well. Well, he likes to wear these flowery dresses over his black jeans and match them or mismatch them or whatever with military shirts and the like yeah?'

'Right.'

'It's been his style for a while and I just kinda followed his lead and started to cross-dress and then . . .

'But Miles doesn't really cross-dress per-se though no?'

'No, not really. He likes to say that the dresses he wears are just supplementary or something, a way of showing that he's an ally and sympathetic to the concerns and causes of the LGBTQ+ community and that he's no yuppie. The hippies now wear black and all that lark. I think he feels a bit guilty for having come from a relatively posh family.'

'So go on.'

'I drunkenly commented a few times that I felt more in touch with my feminine side whenever I wore a dress and Miles and a lot of the girls, many of whom are gay, encouraged me to *go with it* so to speak.'

'Go with it?' asked Bolts.

'Yeah, you know, own it.'

'So you imagined you were Ed Banger?'

'Edweena Banger, or Ed Banger as you say, is no mard arse right?'

'Right,' acknowledged Bolts. 'Not at all.'

'So I wasn't concerned about being ridiculed because I knew that like Edweena, I could call upon my inner masculine reserves if my feminine exterior was ever bullied.'

'But,' said Bolts. 'Most biological women can't do that and have to cultivate different strategies to deal with conflict, so you were never really going to be a full-on female like were you? You know, a *real* woman.'

'What's a real woman?' asked Blister.

> "*And just like a man must be well hung,*
>
> *To be a real woman, you have to be young . . .* 𝄞

'A real woman,' replied Bolts, 'is somebody born with a cunt, you dozy twat.'

'And,' said Blister, 'I suppose that means that a real man is somebody born with a dick, you cunt?'

'Exactly.'

'Are you saying that to transition from one sex to another isn't possible?'

'I'm suggesting mate, that transitioning from one sex to *the* other, not *another*, isn't possible. There are only two sexes, two only. If you don't understand that this is a biological fact and that no matter how many fuckin' communal paroxysms ever take place, this has always been the case and it is impossible to change sex. It's possible to change appearance and to approximate the opposite or complimentary sex or whatever, but it's impossible to actually change. Tell me you get it mate, you daft scrote. Tell me that you appreciate my point of view, which is that there is fuck all wrong with people dressing however they like or imagining that they are a woman or a man when they aren't. The problem is when the government weaponizes it and begins to exploit issues like body dysmorphia for its own benefit and languishes in its own self-aggrandizing morality when it investigates folk with an eye on prosecuting for stating the biological facts that it itself taught us in school.'

'I get it: I got it today, like I say, when Tilly unknowingly threw this puzzled look in my direction. Simply put, no amount of masculine reserves could armor me or shield me from that. I just felt like a proper dickhead. All I've had around here is positive attention. Especially from the females: You wouldn't believe how many supposed lesbians I've shagged since I started dressing that way; how many lonely dykes having had a fight with their partner have knocked on my door pissed at midnight looking for a bit, explaining that they weren't strictly gay and that they'd come to realize that they were in fact non-binary.'

'Lid for every pot,' laughed Bolts.

'I made excuses up in Derby this morning, saying that I needed to get back home because I needed to be in my safe space and that there were too many unmasked people around.'

'Oh yeah?'

'Yeah. But the truth is mate, looking at all them blokes dressed up as woman and all competing with each other to see who could camp-it-up the most and who could sound the most effeminate nauseated me. I wouldn't bother, but none of them were even remotely attractive as their new female incarnations. Every fuckin' one of 'em, including me, hadn't had a wash in days or a fuckin' shave. I went into the toilet this mid-morning for a piss and stood looking at myself in the mirror and just thought, *what a twat; what a right self-fabricated cunt you've turned out to be*. And then when I saw you and I spoke to you, I could hear the cunt in my tone of voice, the dickhead that I'd become, but I fought it off. I fought it off relatively successfully until Tilly involuntarily shot me *that* glance.'

'And so you decided to have a wash?' laughed Bolts.

'And so I decided to have a shower and a shave and to razor my head and to change my clothes and get back to basics: t-shirt, shorts. Next time I go down the plots I'm gonna take everything related to Periwinkle, *Peri-fucking-winkle* for Christ's sake, and burn the job-lot of it.'

'You're done then yeah?'

'Yeah, no more Alan Carr/Chatty Man routine. The world's gone mad Bolts and to be honest, I feel like I just been rescued from the brink. I'm fed-up to the back teeth mate of all this bollocks that's going on because nothing makes sense anymore; d'you know what I mean?'

'I *do* know what you mean pal, I *do* know,' replied Bolts before tugging at Blister's t-shirt. '*Fight the system, fight back.*'

'To be honest Bolts mate, I don't know how to fight back because all in all fighting progressive wokery is like swinging an axe at a swarm of mosquitoes which is probably why so many people just get on board with it so that they can just get on and get by; either that or they keep their mouth shut to avoid any kick back, any retribution. It's hard to fight back when you're surrounded by people who all have the same opinion and who build a lifestyle around that opinion, an opinion which is different from your own.'

'Social Proof mate, it's contagious.'

'What?'

'Social Proof, it's genetically based and culturally transmissible.'

'I'm not with you,' said Blister. 'What're you on about?'

'Hang on a sec,' replied Bolts. 'Let me Google it. Here, it's from Wikipedia this, so there may well be other definitions that are a bit different, but it gives the overall gist –

Social proof is a psychological and social phenomenon wherein people copy the actions of others in an attempt to undertake behavior in a given situation. The term was coined by Robert Cialdini in his 1984 book *Influence*, and the concept is also known as informational social influence.

Social proof is considered prominent in ambiguous social situations where people are unable to determine the appropriate mode of behavior, and is driven by the assumption that the surrounding people possess more knowledge about the current situation.

The effects of social influence can be seen in the tendency of large groups to conform. This is referred to in some publications as the herd behavior. Although social proof reflects a rational motive to take into account the information possessed by others, formal analysis shows that it can cause people to converge too quickly upon a single distinct choice, so that decisions of even larger groups of individuals may be grounded in very little information.

Anyhow, like I say,' concluded Bolts. 'That's the general gist, the overall meat of the meaning.'

12

'I think Marx had a point though Tilly don't you?' said Miles as he was uncorking the Shiraz. 'You know, about the distribution of wealth and about the working-class owning the means of production.'

'You think the working-class as a whole should own the means of production?'

'Well it's different now, but yeah, the disenfranchised.'

'Disenfranchised?'

'People of color, the working-class, women, the LGBTQ+ community, refugees and asylum seekers, immigrants, non-able bodied . . .

'Children of all races?' added Tilly.

'Sure,' said Miles.

'And the elderly?'

'Absolutely.'

'So who's left?'

'The rich.'

'What, like Mohamed Al-Fayed, Mohamed Bin Issa Al Jaber, Alisher Usmanov, Sri and Gopi Hinduja?'

'They don't sound white Tilly,' said Miles.

'What's race got to do with it?'

'Race has got everything to do with it; people of color lack privilege.'

'They're all billionaires living in Britain.'

'So?'

'So d'you believe that their wealth should be taken from them and redistributed to the working-class and others whom you feel are disenfranchised?'

'No, not really, no.'

'How come?'

'Because to sequester the wealth of people of color would be racist.'

'Right,' lied Tilly. 'I see what you mean. You really care about minorities don't you Miles?'

'Not bad this Shiraz,' remarked Miles, not wanting to directly reply, aiming to project modesty, unable to detect any tone of sarcasm. 'Notes of blackcurrant, blueberry, boysenberry, chocolate and oak.'

'All-in-all,' Tilly asked after a thoughtful pause, 'which do think is the more legitimate of causes then Miles, the environmental issues raised by Extinction Rebellion, or the Marxist redistribution of wealth as outlined by prominent members of the United Nations Intergovernmental Panel on Climate Change?'

'They're both equally as valid I'd say,' he said.

'But that guy from the UN-IPCC, Ottmar Edenhofer the German economist, said that climate policy is not about environmental issues and that it's about the redistribution of wealth, so right there within the environmental movement you have an ideological disparity. Those at the top in international governmental organizations are, unsurprisingly, primarily concerned with the economics surrounding climate change while those like supporters of XR who are on the streets and motivated by grassroots activism are fundamentally concerned with what they see as the degradation of the earth and are convinced that there is only a decade or so left before it's too late and the world comes to an end which is why something must be done now, immediately. Right?'

'Licorice too, herbs and olives.'

'Are you listening Miles love?'

'Sorry, yeah, I'm listening.'

'Which Miles, do feel is the more important path to pursue, that proposed by Extinction Rebellion, or the economic doctrine put forth by people like Mr. Edenhofer?'

'Shall we go for a walk?' said Miles ignoring Tilly's question. 'It's a nice enough evening, we could walk along the canal and meet Blister and Bolts on their way back.'

The walk towards the *Thyme & Thistle* was in the opposite direction from the shop that Tilly had visited earlier and they appeared to walking out of town away from any and all buildings and out into the fields and rural Yorkshire proper. An occasional narrowboat passed and the occupants invariably nodded, waved or called out a cordial greeting backed by a self-contented smile. The post-dusk mood was one of pastoral England, of a quaint countryside scene uncluttered by trees, one rather of rolling fields with drystone walls, craftmanship and regional nuance. Away from the digital landscape the world was at peace and Tilly felt enveloped by the overwhelming sense that she was at home here, despite the fact that the objective natural beauty was far less striking than the expansive deserts of Texas or the vast forested regions of Canada. The English countryside thought Tilly, was far less brash and evoked a more subtle appreciation of the natural environment, one which required quiet contemplation due to its comparatively smaller scale. The Texan environment was unfathomably huge but it could be like the oft and undeserved perception of its people, belligerent and brash to the eye, barren, arid and cruel.

'I think,' said Miles, 'I think that maybe what you're saying is true, that the left hand of the environmental movement as characterized by Extinction Rebellion, isn't really aware of what the right hand, as characterized by the United Nations Intergovernmental Panel on Climate Change, is doing. Activists associated with XR appear focused on the national government and what the Tories are or are not doing, and although they would agree with the findings outlined and expressed in the latest (2021) UN-IPCC Assessment Report or what's known as AR6, I'm quite sure that they aren't really aware of what is being said by this German economist guy that you mentioned and that when . . .

'Ottmar Edenhofer,' said Tilly. 'His name's Ottmar Edenhofer.'

'Right. Well anyway, I think a lot of people are supportive of wealth distribution or redistribution, but if what you're saying is true, then a lot of grass roots activists are being misled by bureaucrats embedded in international organizations whose priority seems to be the management of huge sums of money. It's hard to believe that anybody could manipulate such an important cause as the health and future sustainability of the planet for personal financial gain.'

'September 11th?'

'Why? What about it?'

'People do all manner of evil things in the belief that it will benefit their cause yeah? I mean, take those Islamic extremists that flew planes into the Twin Towers, I mean, imagine being faced with the choice of burning to death in a blaze of jet fuel or having to leap out of a hundred and fifth-floor window, either way it's certain death right?'

'Nine-eleven,' declared Miles emphatically, 'was an inside job; I really believe that Tilly.'

'And, for the sake of this conversation and getting my point across, I'm glad you do.'

'Getting your point across?'

'You really believe that it was in inside job?'

'Of course, don't you?'

'I don't know what to believe Miles love if I'm honest.'

'No?'

'No. I'd like to think it was Osama Bin Laden that was behind it and to some degree it would make sense that he was responsible for the organization of those events but the manner in which the Twin Towers came down and the other building, what was it called . . .

'Building 7,' replied Miles. '*7 World Trade Center* it was called, wasn't even directly hit.'

'If I had to bet, and I don't bet, but if I had to, I'd say that Bin Laden was responsible. But you don't, right?'

'Right, I think it was an inside job, I'm sure of it.'

'You think that the American administration of the day planned such a heinous attack on its own country and people?'

'I do, and I'm surprised you don't. I'm surprised every time anybody says that they deny or doubt that it was an inside job, that Bush and his cronies and his father's associates in the Deep State had nothing to do with it and that Bin Laden and Mohamed Atta were responsible.'

Although the sun had set and any insects were now inactive, a few erratic mallards and the occasional languid swan swam in the canal, as dog walkers, strolling elderly couples and the odd couple or trio of cigarette smoking loitering teenagers stood around spitting at the floor between glances at the phone in the palm of their hand.

'You fancy sitting over here?' asked Tilly, pointing to a stream that ran parallel to the canal. 'Wanna sit over there, near that little waterfall what's-it?'

'Nice here,' said Miles a few minutes later when they were sat and settled. 'Comfy. We should have brought some wine.'

'Read your mind,' she replied, pulling the recorked, almost full bottle from her bag. 'No glasses though, so if you want to share the bottle, you'll have to risk catching the coronavirus from me.'

'I'm sure catching covid-19 from you wouldn't be as severe as catching it from Bolts,' he told Tilly, who waited a few seconds for the punchline before suddenly realizing none would be forthcoming, that the remark wasn't a joke and nor was it meant as flattery or intended to be flirtatious, it was just a simple honest comment that Tilly could make neither head nor tail of.

'Then if you believe,' said Tilly, continuing the thread, 'that 9/11 was an inside job, you surely believe that people can do all sorts of evil things because they're sure that it will further their cause, right?'

'Right.'

'And therefore, it's possible that this fella at the UN-IPCC and others like him are pushing the climate narrative in order to further *their* cause?'

'What cause?'

'What was the cause of those *insiders* who pulled the 9/11 *job*?'

'Money,' said Miles. 'Money, power, influence and cronyism. The Old Boys' Club; the Old Boys' Network, nepotism and corruption.'

'And do you think that it's at all possible that there's an Old Boys' Network which is using Climate Change as a way to profit, gain influence and power for itself and its individual constituent members?'

'But,' said Miles, 'we can see the changes in the climate all around us all the time, it's different.'

'Your tattoo right,' said Tilly.

'Yeah, what about it?'

'The Hockey Stick Graph yeah, like we've said, it was perhaps the centerpiece of Al Gore's film *An Inconvenient Truth*, and the book which won him and the UN-IPCC the Nobel Peace Prize in 2007?'

'Right, what about the tattoo, him, them, it?'

'Have you seen the follow-up film, *An Inconvenient Sequel: Truth to Power*?'

'Never heard of it,' said Miles. 'Any good?'

'Didn't gain much traction, like you say, you've never heard of it. There's a clip of him talking about the film in front of a live audience in 2017 which has him explaining that ten years earlier when the first film came out, the most criticized scene was an animated scene showing that the combination of sea-level rise and storm surge would mean that ocean water would end up in the 9/11 Memorial Site which was then being built. People, Gore said, were remarking that that was a terrible exaggeration, then there's footage of just that, flood water rushing down the steps of the memorial.'

'Then how come it didn't get much attention?'

'Because it was a flood which was due to excessive rain rather than rising sea water; it was due to weather and not climate.'

'So what's the difference then between weather, or extreme weather, and climate. Surely, there is no difference and it was right-wing propaganda that resulted in the film not being as successful as the first one and the message prevented from getting out. It's not right Tilly, these people are evil.'

'These people?'

'Yeah, these people: Climate Deniers – capital C / capital D.'

'I don't think that there are serious people with any influence denying that climate exists Miles love.'

'There are enough people denying that the climate is changing due to human activity.'

'Like where?'

'Like here.'

'Britain?'

'Yes, Britain.'

'But the climate hasn't changed, has it?'

'Of course it has, but then again you wouldn't really know since you've been away, so it's no wonder you're doubtful because you haven't seen the changes that have been occurring in the weather these last few years.'

Miles took a slug from the bottle he'd been holding and passed it to Tilly with an affable shrug and a taut smile of resignation as a way of illustrating that his tone was one of passion for his cause rather than disapproval of her line of reasoning because after all, he'd often told himself, explaining to others the importance of awakening to the issue of climate change and the need to act now had become his *raison d'etre* in recent years. Mild-mannered climate Miles the anarcho-punk was well known around town as a reliable ally to everyone, he even lived with his best friend who was male-to-female transitioning. Everybody liked Miles and he liked everyone that was clued-in enough to recognize the absolute urgency with which humanity NOW had to recognize its neglectful behavior of the recent past and the damage done over the past century and a half or so, and which originated in his own back yard in the north west of England in places like Manchester, Bolton, Wigan and Liverpool. He was born in the north west, as too was the industrial revolution, so it was like he was the runt sibling of the imbecilic brainless ogre which had ruined the world and he felt shame, guilt and remorse, and so too he was convinced, should everyone else.

'Everybody,' he told Tilly, 'should be made fully aware of the damage we've done to the planet and we all need to make amends and change our behavior and begin to live different lives with altered priorities so that there is an earth for generations to come.'

'But the climate in Britain hasn't changed Miles love, the weather might be erratic and different from one year to the next but that's only natural right? The weather doesn't follow the Gregorian calendar, so of course the weather on a small island like Britain isn't going to be exactly the same each year. The weather may be different from year to year but the climate hasn't changed: It's not like we can suddenly grow top notch quality grapes in Carlyle, Gateshead or Dundee and . . .' she concluded by raising the bottle of Shiraz and offering it back to Miles, 'produce wine like this.'

'Wine like this?'

'When we can consistently produce wine like this from grapes grown in the north of England and Scotland, then we'll know that there has been a change in the climate. However, most current references to climate change are little other than references to weather. Miles my love, it's a con. Now drink up, I think I can see Bolts and Blister pedaling back this way.'

Part D: Ideologically Unsound . . .

13.

Back on the narrowboat the four resumed their respective seats around the small table in the fore-well and Bolts and Blister each emptied the contents of their particular recent purchases onto small plastic trays that Miles had bought from the pound shop in a rainy Bradford and had cost him a quid for a set of three.

'You been catching up then?' asked Bolts.

'Putting the world to rights,' replied Tilly.

'Oh aye?'

'Yeah,' said Miles. 'Tilly the ecologist doesn't believe that climate change is a crisis and that an increase in CO_2 is apparently a good thing for the planet.'

'Really?' asked Blister. 'An increase in CO_2 is a good thing Tilly?'

'And Miles,' replied Tilly. 'Believes that 9/11 was in an inside job and had nothing to do with Osama Bin Laden.'

'I do too,' said Blister. 'Always have done: follow the money.'

'Exactly,' echoed Miles. 'Always follow the money.'

'Got any scales?' asked Bolts. 'I wanna weigh this weed.'

'I *do* believe that 9/11 was an inside job Tilly, those three buildings fell into their own footprints and are the first ever to collapse due to fire, and three in one day within hours of each other, minutes. It doesn't add up.'

'What do you think Bolts?'

'Not sure till I've weighed it, looks okay but I wanna check to make sure that fella Badger's not on the swizz.'

'What d'you think about 9/11?' clarified Blister, 'Not the weight of the weed.'

'Don't know who did it but you can bet it was about money, power and/or ideology: some megalomaniacal set of shit-heads with a god complex for a dead cert, that's for def.'

'I agree,' concurred Miles, 'that it was about money and power, mostly money.'

Tilly paused for a few seconds as the table went quiet before asking: 'And yet you don't think that those promoting the idea of catastrophic manmade climate change are motivated by financial interests and the vast amounts of money that they can generate for themselves?'

'That 'an all,' said Bolts as he poked the weed around the tray with a teaspoon. 'Have you got any digital kitchen scales Miles mate?'

'We've not no, sorry.'

'Remember earlier Miles?' asked Tilly. 'We were talking about Nick Cohen and his claim that the fossil fuel industry spent billions on propaganda?'

'Yeah?'

'And that it had, this propaganda, been accepted by what he described as "know-nothing elements on the right", had "caused incalculable damage", presumably to the anti-carbon cause?'

'Right.'

'Turns out that those promoting global warming get almost 3,500 times as much funding as the skeptics and a billion dollars a day is being spent around the world to prevent climate change. And, as long as we're talking about money and following it, Al Gore spent 8.8 million dollars on a 6,500-square-foot seafront home in California after preaching to the world that in no time at all, that coastal regions around the globe will be under water and consequently, I would presume, uninhabitable.'

'He what?' laughed Bolts.

'Yeah, that was in 2010 that he bought that after saying, just four years earlier, that coastlines could be twenty feet under water.'

'*Could*,' replied Bolts. 'Always guarding themselves with weasel words like *could* and what not.'

Miles sat back and watched as the former scrap metal collector continued to push the weed around the plastic tray between picking up one bud after another and holding it up to the light before giving it a thoughtful sniff. Tilly could see that Miles wasn't in any rush to reply so decided to busy herself in the galley where Blister was rearranging some cups in a cupboard. Miles couldn't swallow the idea that the movement he'd come to view as the most important of his time was in any way a sham. There was a time back in the seventies and eighties when the primary concern had been the destruction of the earth by nuclear weapons and CND had been the movement to join and to venerate, promote and represent, because politicians back then couldn't be trusted to keep their fingers off the polished red buttons or the dirty green, thought of as pretty.

> ♪ And they didn't teach me that in school, it's something that I learnt on my own:
> That power is measured by the pound or the fist;
> It's as clear as this oh . . .

It was impossible to imagine the unthinkable Miles told himself, as he sat watching the despicable Bolts idle away the lazy seconds, every last one an eternity as long as he remained onboard and in such close proximity to himself and moreover, Tilly. How such ignorance of environmental issues could ever be rewarded with the apparent contentment with which Bolts carried himself was beyond Miles; and how indeed such empty headedness could be found attractive to highly educated females was a fact that greatly eluded Miles. How could a council estate idiot wind up employed as a corporate consultant in Hong Kong or wherever, when he - of although modest, essentially honest middle-class early years - found himself almost penniless and living on a rented barge as he fast approached sixty? It didn't make any sense really until he thought it through and settled on the fact that he was no slave to the system, no nine-to-five drone. He was better, Miles Beta. He was and always had been a rebel, so to begin to doubt himself and his beliefs now made little sense because Extinction Rebellion and his comrades worldwide were the answer to the global degradation wrought by capitalism and fossil fuels, the filth and the poison that was CO_2.

'Y'okay Miles love?' asked Tilly stepping into the fore-well from the galley. 'Penny for your thoughts.'

'I was just admiring Bolts' attention to detail.'

'Oh yeah?'

'What're you doing back there?'

'Just tidying up a bit, before settling in. Don't want to be faced with a stack of dirty pots first thing in the morning.'

'Look at you,' mewled Miles in a tone that grated Tilly's sense of authenticity, the gauge within which tilted her towards accepting something as either genuine or inauthentic, 'all domesticated and responsible.'

'It's with having kids,' laughed Tilly. 'Comes with the territory of motherhood, being a parent.'

Miles thought that Tilly must have been a good mother when her girls were younger and that her plans to go visit them in Texas before relocating to Washington D.C. was more proof that she still was an ideal parent. She'll still be the ideal mother, thought Miles, changing with the times as they grow older.

'Anyhow,' Bolts suddenly declared as he loaded a pipe before scooping the rest of the weed from the tray into an airtight plastic container with a screw-on lid. 'I'd rather live on a boat like this than in some huge high-maintenance yuppie palace out there on the Left-coast with all the yoghurt knitters and Zen-fascists wanting to control you a hundred percent naturally.'

'Yeah?' said Blister. 'Really?'

'And I believe in this, and it's been tested by research,' replied Bolts.

'Why, who's joined the church after fucking nuns?'

'Some of your more extremist underwater basket weavers reside over there.'

'Where?'

'Frisco baby, L.A. and Orange.'

'Like who?'

'J.B. himself, Bad Religion: Nuevo Dead Heads dude.'

Miles interrupted: 'Underwater basket weavers, yoghurt knitters, Zen fascists, Nuevo Dead Heads?'

'Aye,' said Bolts. 'Panic merchants selling doomsday prophesies and disseminating sentiments of self-loathing, guilt and shame among and amid their respective and shared congregations.'

'I'm not with you,' said Blister.

'To be honest,' added Miles. 'Neither am I, if the truth's to be known.'

Bolts tapped Tilly's knee under the table with his own and she reciprocated, though as a way of jokingly telling him to stop rather than in agreement: 'Stop it.'

'They're all in it for the money,' Bolts began to explain. 'The politicians, the pundits in the mainstream media, the majority of the punks, the job-lot really mate. It's a gravy-train and right now it looks like the 11015 Kushinagar Express from Mumbai to Gorakhpur, stacked full to the gills with punters and crowded up-top with just as many looking for a free ride.'

'Seriously?' said Miles. 'That's a bit strong yeah? Bloody hell.'

'You heard of Noam Chomsky Miles mate?'

'Yeah, I have yeah.'

'And you, as an anti-capitalist anarcho-peace-punk appreciate his politics when he says something along the lines of, "The media serve the interests of state and corporate power, which are closely interlinked, framing their reporting and analysis in a manner supportive of established privilege and limiting debate and discussion accordingly"? You're on board with that yeah Miles?'

'If Chomsky said it, yeah. 'Yeah, of course I'm on board with that.'

'When,' replied Bolts, 'the legacy media, the entertainment industry and Hollywood, the governments of the Anglosphere, most of your peers, the big multinational companies, big tech, and the vast majority of punks who ever comment on such issues and your punk rock pals are promoting the woke paradigm including critical race theory, child gender transitioning, climate change hyperbole and universal vaccination, making an analogy to the overcrowded Mumbai Express and a gravy train is what in your book?'

'I can't bring myself to believe that these people don't care for the downtrodden and suffering around the world Bolts and that they're just on the gravy train and in it for the money, can you Tilly? Pez?'

Blister ignored being referred to as Pez and said: 'I can believe that politicians are in it for the money; that is, they support a cause or promote a cause or whatever in the interest of lining their own pockets, of course I can.'

'And you Tilly?'

'Sure, politicians the world over promote causes which will benefit themselves, their political interests and any Old Boys' Network they might well be a part of, sure.'

'And punk bands?' asked an incredulous Miles. 'Really?'

'What like,' began Bolts as he lit the pipe, 'you think that punk bands and punks in general are above having the wool pulled over their eyes and are incapable of being morally compromised?'

'Exxon gave way more money to organizations concerned about environmental degradation due to global warming resulting from the claim that there is too much CO_2 than they did to skeptics. The environmental movement is awash with funding from governments, big business and philanthropists and is widely supported by thousands of journalists which act as cheerleaders for their cause, the cause which ignores the plight of the poor and needy around the world. Not long ago, an independent news outlet in Canada got hold of a list which named almost fifteen hundred news outlets - not journalists because that would mean many more - which collectively were recipients of tens of millions of dollars. As recipients of large sums of money, those outlets are expected to toe-the-Trudeau-line and support the policies of the Canadian Prime Minister's party yeah?'

'I suppose,' said Miles. 'I suppose that if they do take the money that there is an expectation to toe-the-line. But isn't that bribery, collusion and corruption? Surely it is right?'

'Hard to really believe that so many journalists could be so readily influenced,' said Blister. 'Difficult to sincerely appreciate that corruption on such a scale could be right in front of peoples' faces and they wouldn't be able to see it.'

'You can't see it if you don't know about it, and when it is brought to light due to a Freedom of Information request, the paid off media just ignores it or plays it down,' replied Tilly. 'I mean Miles love, you say that you're a anarcho-communist yeah right?'

'Right,' replied Miles.

'Well then, is there anything inside you that might even remotely prompt you to suspect that capitalism is possible of being corrupted?'

'Of course.'

'Then why not in this instance?'

'Because 97% of all scientists believe that the earth is in trouble due to manmade global warming, it's simple. Numbers don't lie and neither does science.'

'He has a point,' said Blister looking at Bolts. 'Despite your little trick on the bus earlier today, I still think he has a point: Science doesn't lie and neither do the numbers.'

'What trick?' asked Tilly.

Blister explained what had happened on the bus with the post-it notes and the questions and Bolts' suggestion, or was it an accusation, that he was predictable and that his opinions on various subjects were little other than platitudes: overly used phrases that he'd been nudged into accepting, internalizing, and repeating.

Miles sat and silently communed with APONI: "Dearest APONI, save me from the ignorance of my sisters Tilly and Periwinkle and the infidel that is Bolts, bless the former two and curse the latter in the name of all that is sacred in the spirit world and here on this ball of filth named earth; hear my plea and help me to effectively remonstrate on behalf of our planet."

'Y'okay Miles mate,' asked Tilly offering him the pipe that she'd just hit after receiving it from Bolts. 'Peace-pipe? Care to commune with the spirits?'

'Go on then,' he replied, seeing it as a sign from APONI. 'Who's next?'

'I am,' said Blister. If there's any left.'

∞

At this there was a short silence which Bolts broke by passing the plastic container across the table towards Blister and saying, 'Help yourself mate,' before turning to Miles and asking, 'D'you know who Liz Truss is?'

'Tory yeah, a Boris bitch conservative.'

'That's right,' replied Bolts. 'Tory MP for South West Norfolk who until recently served as Minister for Women and Equalities before being moved over in the reshuffle to the office of the Secretary of State for Foreign, Commonwealth and Development Affairs.'

'Foreign Secretary?' said Tilly.

'Aye,' said Bolts.

'What about her?' asked Miles.

'Not really about her, more really about what was said about her.'

'In the papers?'

'Jonathon Pie, you know that guy?'

'I do yeah,' said Miles. 'Funny: witty.'

'He is yeah. Anyhow, in one of his typical videos where he faces the camera but is speaking to his producer . . .

'Tim?'

'Yeah Tim, Tim the producer. Well, he mentions that Liz Truss has been moved in the reshuffle over at Number Ten from being the Minister for Women and Equalities to being the Secretary of State, which can only ever be seen as a promotion.'

'And?' asked Tilly.

'And anyhow, Jonathon Pie goes on to take the right royal piss out of the fact that she's been promoted to such a high level and prominent position in the government where she'll often have to function as the face of Britain on the world stage after being filmed in the House of Commons declaring that drones illegally delivering drugs to a prison were scared away by guard dogs, or watch dogs, or whatever and . . .

'How,' asked Miles, 'can drones be frightened away by barking dogs? Drones are inanimate objects with no emotions like fear to influence. That's why I like Johnathon Pie, he just points out the obvious.'

'Right,' added Blister. 'That's why I like him too; he's really good at taking the piss out of idiots.'

'Who are the idiots?' asked Tilly.

'Liz Truss for one,' replied Miles. 'And anybody else who believes that a drone could be scared away by barking dogs.'

'Spot on,' said Blister. 'Dick heads.'

'Bolts?' asked Tilly.

'I'm saying nowt,' he replied, looking at his watch. 'How long before the penny drops.'

'What penny?' asked Blister.

'Can I?' asked Tilly.

'Aye,' said Bolts. 'Go on then.'

'Jonathon Pie,' began Tilly, 'has a great sense of humor right?'

'Right,' said Blister.

'Yeah?' said Miles.

'Well, to be honest, I'm not one-hundred-percent sure what his intent was, but I bet I can guess.'

'Guess what?'

'Did you check out the comments Bolts?'

'I did yeah, and many of them were unironically in agreement with him and the point of view he expressed when he accused Liz Truss of being unsuitable for the job.
'

'The thing is,' said Blister, 'there's no way that she's up for the job if she believes that drones are afraid of dogs, she's just out of her depth and gullible.'

'Spot on,' said Miles, gullible is the word. 'Inexperienced and wet behind the ears, no ability to sort the wheat from the chaff which as Foreign Secretary is a required fundamental skill.'

'She wasn't talking about drones being afraid of dogs,' replied Bolts, 'as much as she was pointing out the fact that when the drone operators saw, through its fitted camera, that the dogs had spotted it and therefore alerted the prison guards by barking. The drone was attempting to deliver drugs to inmates at a prison and the drone operators decided not to make the drop once they realized that it'd been clocked by the guards who had been alerted to its presence because the dogs were looking up in the sky and barking their yeds off.'

'And,' said Tilly, 'a lot of people were eager to jump on the band wagon and label Liz Truss as being unsuitable for the job, which she may well be, though not for the reasons levelled at her for supposedly saying that drones are scared of dogs. Whether or not Jonathon Pie was being sarcastic and trolling his own audience is up for discussion but the thing is, as I'm sure can be seen in the comments section of the video, a lot of anti-Tories will have bought the false narrative of her believing that drones were scared of dogs. The point is, lies and twisted stories can be found in all genres of media in this day and age. Hyperbole and exaggeration are everywhere.'

'And the sea tastes like petrol?' asked Miles.

'Exactly,' said Tilly.

'I recently saw this interview with Jello Biafra from the Dead Kennedys,' said Bolts. 'Jello said that both Klaus Fluoride the bass player and East Bay Ray the guitarist were ten to twelve years older than him and already in their thirties when they formed the band in the late 70's but the truth is, Klaus is eight years older, not ten or twelve, and Ray is five months to the day younger than Jello: Jello was born on June 17th 1958 and Ray on November 17th of the same year.'

'So?' asked Miles. 'So what?'

'He's known these people for over forty years and can't remember how old they are? Bollocks. It may be that his memory is failing him and if that's the issue, I feel sorry for the guy because that band was one of the best back in the day. Anyhow, later in the interview he claims that Brexit grew out of the British National Front and that Enoch Powell had been its leader: Bollocks again.'

'So people like Jonathan Pie and Jello Biafra make mistakes and then . . .

'But we don't know whether they purposefully made mistakes in order to mislead or whether they accidentally made mistakes which are misleading. Either way, what they say needs to be addressed. If they misled on purpose, they are malicious and if they accidentally misled, they're not fit for purpose. At least not fit for purpose when it comes to being a reliable source of accurate information.'

'But what does it matter?' asked Blister, 'If Jello Biafra can't remember exactly how old his former band mates are or whether or not Jonathon Pie is trolling his own audience or not?'

'It doesn't really matter, though it serves as a poignant analogy because each has quite a big platform and can potentially influence tens of thousands, if not hundreds of thousands of people. The main point,' continued Tilly, 'is that politicians and others in far more influential positions can have a huge impact on the direction that public opinion is steered, due to cognitive degeneration, sheer laziness or by using ethically questionable tactics.'

'Drones are scared of dogs,' said Blister after a short pause. 'I can't believe you fell for that Miles.

'You too,' replied Miles good naturedly enough as he nodded at Pez. 'It wasn't just me.'

14

'Later in the video,' continued Bolts, 'Biafra says that Donald Trump is the biggest threat to world peace and . . .

'Wait,' said Tilly. 'When was this interview.'

'Yeah when?' said Blister.

'September 25th 2020.

'And how d'you remember that?' asked Miles.

'Day before my dad's birthday.'

'Really?'

'Yeah. Anyhow, later in the video he says that Trump was the biggest threat to world peace, but that Bolsonaro in Brazil was maybe more of a menace because he's a bigger threat to any kind of hope of turning the tide against, not merely climate change he emphasizes, but climate collapse. The interviewer agrees and then remarks that the Amazon is burning to death right now. For many punks around the world, interviews like this are what they regard as an alternative source of news and information, one which is reliable and worth sharing, repeating and building an identity around, a movement and a way of life. There was a time when I thought that the opinions of Jello Biafra and the songs of Dead Kennedy, Dick Lucas from Subhumans, Citizen Fish and Culture Shock and their output, and Crass and many of the bands that they influenced, expressed legitimate alternative points of view, but not no more. These days you can buy a UK Subs face mask for 8 quid or one from Crass for 9, or Crass cufflinks for 27 pound fifty a pair, cufflinks for fuck's sake. Anarcho-punk cufflinks!'

Miles the anarcho-communist began to remonstrate by pointing out that Steve Ignorant, one of the two original founding members of the band who was behind the website which sold Crass cufflinks, socks, beanie hats and other items, was simply making a few quid and that there was nothing at all unethical about doing so. Bolts on the other hand countered by mentioning that the band had made money from songs which declared, "Yes that's right, punk is dead, just another cheap product for the consumer's head", and that it was the hypocrisy which amused him and not the making of a few quid that in any way troubled or bothered him. Bolts also pointed out that in their song, *It's the Greatest Working Class Rip Off* from their fourth L.P., *Christ: The Album*, they'd admonished other punk bands and practiced hypocrisy themselves when they sang --

> Punk is dead you wankers, cos you killed it through and through
> In your violent world of chaos, what you gonna do?
> Is Top of the Pops the way in which you show how much you care?
> You take off now to the U.S.A. and spread your message there?

It was insincere and sanctimonious regarding the *In your violent world of chaos* remark because the other founding member, Penny Rimbaud, was on record recalling that in the early days, they would hand out pamphlets which gave instructions on both how to bake your own bread *and* build your own bombs. Then there was the reference to bands appearing on Top of the Pops and apparently selling out by going over to play live in America, which Crass did anyway: Miles remained unconvinced.

'I'm not too sure,' said Miles, 'If you don't mind me saying . . .

'Yeah?' replied Bolts, sensing his apprehension. 'No, I don't mind at all.'

'Thing is though right, I couldn't help but notice that you've got a Crass badge on your backpack, so aren't you the hypocrite?'

'I like Crass and what they did in the late 70's and early 80's for punk and for what they meant to a lot of working-class kids on estates up and down England, how they brought up issues of animal rights and women's rights and unnecessary class division, racial concerns, religious indoctrination. I liked all that stuff, and I liked the music and still do. I'll always think of them as one of the most important bands of my coming-of-age years, our coming-of-age years, but that doesn't mean that one or two of their members haven't been hypocrites or that Jello Biafra is an expert on geo-political issues or that Dick Lucas is a reliable source of information when it comes to the subject of catastrophic anthropogenic climate change.'

'Anthropo-what?' asked Blister.

'Anthropogenic,' replied Tilly in a tone intended to avoid sounding condescending. 'Manmade.'

'Oh right, is that what it's called: Anthropogenic?'

'I still play their tunes regularly,' said Bolts, 'but none of the bands we've just been on about are legitimate or reliable resources when it comes to climate change, and neither are organizations like Extinction Rebellion.'

'Then what is a reliable and legitimate source,' asked Blister sarcastically.

Bolts looked at Tilly who then said, 'There are many reliable and legitimate sources, it's just that you'll seldom, if at all ever, hear them via the mainstream media, which – at least in Canada – appears to have been bought off.'

'How many news outlets did you say had been paid off?' asked Miles, attempting to suddenly sound concerned and sympathetic because after all, Tilly had been a taxpayer in Canada for three decades or so.

'Yeah,' added Blister. 'And how many millions were spent by the Canadian government in handouts to these media outlets and journalists and others that they employed?'

'The list is of almost 1,500 media outlet companies and collectively they received sixty-one million dollars in what was termed *pre-election emergency relief.*'

Bolts whistled at the sum of money then asked: 'Sixty-one million dollars?'

'That's right,' replied Tilly. 'Sixty-one million dollars of tax-payers hard-earned money went through the fingers of the government and into the coffers of almost fifteen hundred media outlets as pre-election emergency relief, and what do you know, these very same media outlets appear to *coincidently* agree with government policies across the board on covid-19 measures, vaccinations and yes, climate change policy.'

'People should wear masks though,' said Miles. 'I do agree with any government that mandates the wearing of masks in public.'

'You believe that masks are effective Miles love?' asked Tilly.

'I do yeah.'

'You wear a mask because you think that it will provide protection against contracting the virus?'

'Yeah, like I say, I do.'

'Then if you believe that your mask is effective in protecting you from catching the virus, why would you need me to wear one because after all, like you just twice said, you're protected by your own mask right?'

'Well yeah, right, I am protected by my own mask but it's a matter of courtesy, isn't it?'

'So it's not about science, it's about courtesy?'

'I suppose.'

'It's about social convention then and compliance and us all being in it together because if you wear a mask and others don't, it'll distinguish you from them and there'll be an us and them scenario?'

'Something like that I suppose,' shrugged Miles before shrugging again with a resigned smile. 'I guess.'

'Masks,' said Bolts. 'They're used to remind us of an alleged virus and to keep the fear hovering in the air; they're fuck all but tools of propaganda.'

'And vaccinations?' pressed Tilly.

'Well, I've had two plus the booster, and I'll get a fourth if one is recommended,' replied Miles.

'You think everybody should get what is referred to as fully vaccinated, two and a booster?'

'Yeah, don't you?'

'You believe that everybody must get vaccinated?' asked Tilly.

'Yeah,' repeated Miles. 'Don't you? I mean, I don't see why the vaccinated people should have to go out in public and have to sit next to unvaccinated people and put themselves at risk, it's just selfish. To be honest, I do agree with the idea that people who haven't been vaccinated shouldn't be allowed to fully participate in society. You know, fly, travel on public transportation in general, attend large events or to be honest, even go to the pub and mingle with vaccinated people. It's too much of a risk; it's inconsiderate, selfish, potentially deadly and something must be done. The government needs to act Tilly, the sooner the better.'

'But Miles love, didn't you get vaccinated to protect yourself?'

'Of course.'

'And if I got it too, it would be to protect myself?'

'Right.'

'How is it that you need me to get vaccinated in order for your vaccination to be effective?'

'The jab,' said Miles, 'doesn't prevent anybody from getting or giving the virus, it just reduces the symptoms, lessons the impact so that the illness is not as bad and people don't have to go into hospital and overwhelm the NHS.'

'Then it's not a vaccination in the traditional sense yeah? It doesn't provide immunity; it just reduces the severity of the symptoms which would make it a medical procedure as opposed to a vaccine that provides immunity. I think if these reputed vaccines were promoted as such, as treatments as opposed to vaccines, people would feel less misled and therefore be all that more receptive to having the jabs.'

'Then again,' said Blister, 'asymptomatic people can pass on the virus right?'

'Isn't the virus spread through coughing and sneezing from an infected person though?' asked Bolts. 'I don't get it. How can the virus be spread if there are no symptoms?'

'Question,' said Tilly, 'for you and Miles.'

'Yeah?' said Blister, 'Go on.'

'How d'you feel about us being here now and me not being fully vaccinated? I mean, I've only had the one, do you feel at all vulnerable?'

'Not really,' replied Blister.

'Same,' added Miles. 'No, not particularly.'

'What I'd like to know,' said Bolts, 'is why people are saying, "*you* need to get a vaccine that doesn't work, so the vaccine that *I* got that doesn't work, will work"

'I'd rather not talk about it to be honest,' said Miles.

'Oh yeah?'

'Yeah. We've got limited time together here today and all we've done is talk about problems; climate change and now the coronavirus and to be honest, I just don't know enough about the subject. I don't mind us exchanging our differences on climate change because I think it's obvious that we have a problem and that we need to act now, whereas with things like masks and jabs it's different. There's too much uncertainty in the air, people are scared.'

'How so?' asked Tilly. 'How d'you mean it's different.'

'Like I say,' said Miles. 'I don't really want to talk about vaccines and masks and what not, because if unvaccinated people die then it's just nature and climate change thinning out the population and . . .

'You think there's a direct link between climate change and the coronavirus, that covid-19 is a symptom of sorts of catastrophic manmade climate change?'

'I do Tilly,' said Miles, but I don't want to talk about it because too many people I know have been affected, or I suspect will be.'

15

'Too many people?' asked Blister.

'Like I say,' repeated Miles with a degree of impatient emphasis. 'I don't really want to talk about it as I don't want to antagonize because all in all, if I'm honest, the denial of the need to wear a mask, social distance, self-isolate, lockdown, get fully vaccinated and be honest about the impact of climate change, including its relationship with covid-19, is bigoted and racist because the coronavirus and climate change adversely affect women, minorities and people of color *far* more than they do straight white men. It's time to act and time to acknowledge that we have to change and relinquish some of our freedoms and that we're going to have to get used to living in a different type of world . . .

'A new kind of England?' asked Bolts.

'Absolutely,' replied Miles. 'We're going to have to reevaluate some things about the would-be freedoms we feel so attached to and make manifest a new kind of freedom.'

'And where do we start?' asked Tilly.

'We start,' said Miles, 'by forcing the government to meet our three demands: Firstly, the government should tell the truth about the predicament we're in due to catastrophic manmade climate change; secondly, commit to net zero carbon emissions by 2025; thirdly, we want the government to form a Citizens' Assembly that it will genuinely listen to and whose recommendations it will then subsequently act upon. If we don't act now as a nation, as a species, our offspring will suffer and that is the biggest act of hypocrisy and Naziism that any human could ever commit, to bring children into the world and then to neglect to provide for them a future full of hope.'

'But didn't you say that humans are a disease upon the planet? Asked Tilly. 'Why,' she teased. 'Why would you be concerned about future generations if you believe that people are nothing more than a virus on the planet, a cosmic disease of sorts?'

'Yeah but, no,' said Miles. 'You know what I mean.

'Go on then . . .

'Not long ago,' interjected Bolts. 'I read this article in *The Guardian* that said a Trade Union members' protest against mandatory vaccine policy in Melbourne wasn't in fact union members expressing their disagreement with union bosses who appeared to be siding with the government, and that it was in fact right-wing Nazi infiltrators.'

'Well,' said Tilly with a laugh. '*The Guardian* wouldn't want its readership or the wider population to think that there was any kind of discord within the ranks of the left and there was ideological division between the union boss government shills and the hard-working union members whose membership dues pay their wages, would they? The left that we belonged to years ago thinks that all it has to do is call somebody right-wing or a Nazi and they've won the debate: argument in the bag, nothing more to say.'

'And your point?' laughed Blister.

'Anyhow, my point is,' replied Bolts with a smile, 'These days, each of these two so-called rebellious punks are peddling the mandatory jab line that's being rolled out by the Tory government they despise. When mandates are put into place which say that an individual no longer has the right to decide what goes into their own body, fascism is at work. That's authentic Nazi behavior: when a fascist action IS done. Thing is though right, calling folk a Nazi for NOT doing something'll probably do any environmentalist cause or group or organization more harm than good. Believe it or not, I'm on your side. I've been vegan since 1982 and I haven't driven a car once since 1996, that's twenty-five years man. Calling people shitty and childish names will do us no good and Extinction Rebellion's antics of gluing themselves to this, that an' t'other's only going to put folk off their message because people have died due to their actions, died because XR blocked roads and sick folk couldn't get to hospital on time. Then you've got this other shower-of-shite talking about, what is it, Insulate Britain? And the number-one idiot causing much of the bother hasn't even insulated his own home: Hypocrites with a cause mate, they're everywhere. They're down the pub and in your tribute bands, they're in your original hardcore and anarcho-punk bands too and in the news and the government's riddled with them and now they're crawling around the fuckin' streets gluing themselves to the tarmac, 'kin dickheads.'

'I suppose,' said Miles. 'Maybe you're right, but something has to be done. It's, like I keep saying, the future generations I feel sorry for the most. That's what I worry about.'

'Listen to this Miles,' said Bolts, just listen to these wise words from MINISTRY's Al Jourgensen: "I mean, it's just, like, 'People. Really?' Look, even if the government is microchipping us and we're all gonna have alien DNA and all that, at least we're all gonna go down together. But in the meanwhile, let's not make each other sick. Just go get your damn vax. I've had mine for months. I'm even gonna get a booster before I go on tour. I wanna make sure that I don't infect people and people don't infect me. It's not a hundred percent accurate, as nothing in this world or universe is, but just do it, please, so we can have our lives back, our entertainment back".'

'So what?' said Miles.

'The bloke can't stand not having his sycophants be able to worship him and his cronies while he's up there on stage and he's like a lot of musicians, which is soaked to the gills in their own need for attention, whether it's on stage, backstage or out and about. The words to the music often mean nothing at all and are fuck all but unnecessary trinkets to dress up their image, like stripes on a sock attempting to increase the durability and function of work boots. The attention they get is narcissistic supply and without it, they feel injured and incomplete. Most musicians, including those in punk bands, are narcissists and by definition self-obsessed. *And anyhow*, why are you all of a sudden concerned about "the kids" and future generations if you feel that the human race is fuck all but a disease on the planet?'

Tilly shook he head a little and a wry smile crept across her face, but Miles didn't appear to notice as Bolts remarked: 'And what's the best way to protect the welfare of the next generation, have no kids? That's what some folks are saying.'

'Kids are being used all over the place to further this idea that the world is in deep trouble, and we need to change our behavior now,' said Tilly. 'It's been going on for a long time now and there's something sinister about it if you ask me. A lot of

136

scientists are saying that the science is NOT in, but *that* side of the story gets downplayed and anybody expressing such a view, no matter how qualified, is labelled as a denier, oftentimes by those who are nowhere near qualified to know whether the science is in, and that human activity is leading to catastrophic manmade climate change. *Denier* is the word used for those who claim that the Holocaust never happened, and such individuals or organizations are consequently labelled as being far-right, fascists and Nazis, accused of being Hitler sympathizers. Similarly, anybody daring to question the narrative that the science is in and that humans are responsible for catastrophic climate change are smeared as deniers and therefore equated with Hitler and the Nazis, which is course ridiculous because the job and role of scientists is to continuously question everything from every which direction in order to prove something as being conclusively correct, and they are not being allowed to speak on certain issues right now in certain circles and on a number of platforms.'

'Like who?' asked Miles as gingerly as he knew how, sensing now that Tilly was becoming irritated and impatient as he supposed she might, given that she was the one with a doctorate in ecology while he and Blister hadn't gone beyond high school and Bolts was schooled in god-knows-what but not ecology, thank fuck.

'This has been going on a long time though yeah Miles love,' said Tilly, 'and it's been well documented in the media over the past fifty years or more, if not before.'

'I've heard of this,' replied Miles. 'And while I'm sure there's some truth in what you're saying, I doubt you could show me anything or tell me anything that would change my mind. I'm with XR: We have to act now.'

'Well,' said Tilly, tilting her tablet towards Miles. 'Read this and tell me what you think.'

'**Already**,' began Miles, '**Too Late. Dire Famine Forecast by '75. By George Getze, Los Angeles Times writer. Los Angles — It is already too late for the world to avoid a long period of famine, a Stanford biologist said Thursday.**

Paul Ehrlich said the "time of famines" is upon us and will be at its worst and most disastrous in 1975.

He said the population of the United States is already too big, that birth control may have to be accomplished by making it involuntary and by putting sterilizing agents into staple foods and drinking water, and that the Roman Catholic Church should be pressured into going along with routine measures of population control.'

'Well then,' asked Tilly. 'What do you think?'

'Already Too Late'

Dire Famine Forecast by '75

By George Getze

Los Angeles Times Writer

LOS ANGELES — It is already too late for the world to avoid a long period of famine, a Stanford University biologist said Thursday.

Paul Ehrlich said the "time of famines" is upon us and will be at its worst and most disastrous by 1975.

He said the population of the United States is already too big, that birth control may have to be accomplished by making it involuntary and by putting sterilizing agents into staple foods and drinking water, and that the Roman Catholic Church should be pressured into going along with routine measures of population control.

Ehrlich said experts keep saying the world food supply will have to be tripled to feed the six or seven billion people they expect to be living in the year 2000.

"That may be possible theoretically but it is clear that it is totally impossible in practice," he said.

Ehrlich spoke at a science symposium at the University of Texas. The text of his speech was made available here.

Since, in Ehrlich's opinion, it is of no longer any use trying to avoid the coming world famines, the best thing to do now is to look past the "time of famines" and hope to have a second chance to control world population sometime in the future.

"At the moment it is shockingly apparent that the battle to feed humanity will end in a rout," Ehrlich said.

He said we have to hope that the world famines of the next 20 years will not lead to thermonuclear war and the extinction of the human species.

"We must assume man will get another chance, no matter how little he deserves one," he said.

From: *The Salt Lake Tribune* - 17th November, 1967.

'When's that from?' asked Blister.

'1967,' replied Miles, followed by a scathing *harrumph* of displeasure. 'November 17th.'

'Jesus,' said Bolts. 'I read his book *The Population Bomb* in the early nineties; didn't know that about twenty-five year earlier he were calling for involuntary population control by putting sterilizing agents into staple foods and the water supply.'

'I've read his book too,' said Tilly. 'A couple of times over the years for one class or another.'

'Yeah but that's population control,' insisted Miles. 'It has nothing to do with the issues that we're facing today with the coronavirus or climate change and extreme weather events, does it?'

'More than once I've read that there's a link between what's termed as the climate crisis and overpopulation.'

'It does show though,' said Bolts. 'Just how long the media has been running with these yarns and giving panic peddling journalists and their rags more time than they really deserve, especially now. These days the mainstream media, or what's now more often known as the legacy media, have a lot more competition to deal with than they ever did in the past. The Internet has taken over things like T.V., radio and hard-copy print journalism, and independent content creators who work out of their kitchen or garage are seeing as much traffic as the big names, more in fact.'

'Maybe,' shrugged Miles. 'What do you think Blister?'

16.

'You got any more examples there on your tablet?' asked Blister as a way of responding.

'Got dozens,' replied Tilly. 'Here, check out the next one.'

'The next article is from two years later in 1969 but it's about the same guy, Dr. Paul R. Ehrlich at Stamford.'

'Read it out will you Blister love?'

'Okay. It says, **PALO ALTO, Calif., Aug. 5 — "The trouble with almost all environmental problems," says Paul R. Ehrlich, the population biologist, "is by the time we have enough evidence to convince people, your dead".'**

'Dickhead,' scoffed Bolts. 'They've been printing that doomsday shite for over fifty year? Wankers.'

'Carry on Blister will you?' asked Tilly. 'There's a bit more isn't there?'

'There is: **While Dr. Ehrlich is gathering that evidence in his laboratory at Stanford University, he is wasting no time trying to convince people that drastic action is needed to head off what he sees as a catastrophic explosion fueled by runaway population growth, a limited world food supply, and contamination of the planet by man. We must realize that unless we are extremely lucky, everybody will disappear in a cloud of blue steam in 20 years.'**

THE NEW YORK TIMES
SUNDAY, AUGUST 10, 1969

FOE OF POLLUTION SEES LACK OF TIME

Asserts Environmental' Ills Outrun Public Concern

By ROBERT REINHOLD
Special to The New York Times

PALO ALTO, Calif., Aug. 5 — "The trouble with almost all environmental problems," says Paul R. Ehrlich, the population biologist, "is that by the time we have enough evidence to convince people, you're dead."

While Dr. Ehrlich is gathering that evidence in his laboratory at Stanford University, he is wasting no time trying to convince people that drastic action is needed to head off what he foresees as a catastrophic explosion fueled by runaway population growth, a limited world food supply, and contamination of the planet by man.

"We must realize that unless we are extremely lucky, everybody will disappear in a cloud of blue steam in 20 years," the 37-year-old scientist said during a coffee break at his laboratory. "The situation is going to get continuously worse unless we change our behavior."

From: *The New York Times* – 10th August, 1969.

'A cloud of blue steam?' asked Blister. 'What's he on about?'

'He means that the coming ice-age that he believed was about to manifest twenty years down the line would result in a loss of crops and therefore famine would become widespread.'

'Never happened though, did it.

17

'Pass the tablet on,' said Tilly. 'We can read one each and decide for ourselves whether or not the media has been aggressively spreading climate hysteria and . . .

'Here, pass it here,' said Bolts. 'Let's have a sken eh?'

'When's this next one from?' asked Blister.

'It's from *The Boston Globe* in 1970 mate.'

'What does it say?'

'Says here, it says, **Scientist predicts a new ice-age by the 21st century . . .**

'Yeah?'

'Yeah, then it goes, **Air pollution may obliterate the sun and cause a new ice-age in the first third of the next century if population continues to grow and earth's resources are consumed at the present rate, a pollution expert predicted yesterday.**'

'Not really on track are we, not for seeing that scenario come to fruition. I wonder where that guy got his funding from,' remarked Blister with a sigh, 'and how much he was given and who by. Makes you think though don't it? Makes you wonder?'

'Does that mate,' replied Bolts. 'What's reckon Miles.

'I don't know what to think.'

The Boston Globe   Thursday, April 16, 1970

Scientist predicts a new ice age by 21st century

Air pollution may obliterate the sun and cause a new ice age in the first third of the next century if population continues to grow and the earth's resources are consumed at the present rate, a pollution expert predicted yesterday.

James P. Lodge Jr. also warned that if the current rate of increase in electric power generation continues, the demands for cooling water will boil dry the entire flow of the rivers and streams of continental United States.

Looking into his "smoggy crystal ball," Lodge also warned that by the next century "the consumption of oxygen in combustion processes, world-wide, will surpass all of the processes which return oxygen to the atmosphere."

Lodge, a scientist at the national center for Atmospheric Research in Boulder, Colo., said the nation's states, with the exception of Alaska and Hawaii, "are already consuming more oxygen than their own green plants replace and that we are importing the balance from the neighboring oceans."

Lodge, speaking at the Institute of Environmental Sciences, at the Sheraton Boston, said three factors could prevent these disasters: population control, a less wasteful standard of living, and a major technological breakthrough in the way man consumes the earth's resources.

From: *The Boston Globe* – 16th April, 1970.

144

18

'My turn?' asked Miles.

'Here you go mate,' said Bolts. 'I think it's that Ehrlich fella again.'

'October 6th this one,' said Miles having taken the tablet and had a glance. '1970: *Redlands Daily Facts* this is from.'

'Go on, what does it say?'

'It reads, **Dr. Ehrlich outspoken ecologist, to speak. Giving aspirins to cancer victims is what Dr. Paul R. Ehrlich thinks of current proposals for pollution control. No real action has been taken to save the environment, he maintains. And it does need saving. Ehrlich predicts that: The oceans will be as dead as Lake Erie in less than a decade:** Blah, blah, blah. Then it says, **America will be subject to water rationing by 1974 and food rationing by 1980.**'

'Do you remember America being subject to food rationing in 1980?' asked Tilly.

'I've never been to America,' replied Miles. 'I don't really know much about the place, but in the final paragraph it says that Ehrlich is the **hero of the ecology movement**.'

Redlands
Daily Facts

REDLANDS, CALIFORNIA, TUESDAY, OCTOBER 6, 1970

Dr. Ehrlich, outspoken ecologist, to speak

"Giving aspirins to cancer victims" is what Dr. Paul R. Ehrlich thinks of current proposals for pollution control. No real action has been taken to save the environment, he maintains.

And it does need saving. Ehrlich predicts that:

The oceans will be as dead as Lake Erie in less than a decade.

The DDT in our fatty tissues has reached levels high enough to cause brain damage and cirrhosis of the liver.

America will be subject to water rationing by 1974 and food rationing by 1980.

University of California Extension, Riverside and World Affairs Council of Inland Southern California will present the outspoken author of "The Population Bomb" and the hero of the ecology movement tomorrow at 8 p.m. He will speak in the gymnasium on the UCR campus.

DR. PAUL EHRLICH

From: *Daily Redlands Facts* – 6th October, 1970.

'Of course he was a hero,' quipped Bolts. 'Especially in the eyes of the media: He kept coming up with these Armageddon type yarns that they could use to sell newspapers. The media loved the guy because bad news sells; we've been laughing about that since we were kids. The news on the telly was always bad and the weather man could never get a forecast right is what we laughed about a lot back in the seventies before we were even teenagers, before there was punk records to complain and to criticize society.'

'What's weirder,' said Blister. 'Is that business about giving aspirin to cancer victims. He was off his head that guy, just thought that sick people should die or what so that the population would be thinned out? Is that what he was on about? 'Kin well creepy that if that's what he was suggesting.'

'But he was a hero,' Bolts sarcastically replied. 'He was, and probably still is, loved by the eco-freaks. Miles?'

'Never heard of him.'

'But do you not see a pattern Miles love. There's definitely a similarity between what was going on then over fifty years ago and what's happening now with the likes of Extinction Rebellion, Greta Thunberg, Insulate Britain and God knows how many other outfits that want the government to impose stricter rules that would severely set us back in the name of progress.'

'Set us back?' asked Miles.

'Well,' said Tilly. 'Let me ask you: Do you think that people in Africa, South America and parts of Asia should be able to develop their countries in the same way that the West has?'

'Of course.'

'But the West developed with the use of coal, natural gas and well, fossil fuels. Should those countries get to use fossil fuels and put the so-called pollutant CO_2 into the atmosphere?'

'I'm not sure really.'

'Should Africans,' pressed Tilly, 'and South Americans, be permitted to use fossil fuels in order to develop their economies and therefore lift themselves out of poverty and all the misery that comes with it? You know, in the same manner that China has done over the past four-or-so decades?'

'Comes with what?' asked Miles.

'Poverty.'

'Why are you picking on Miles?' asked Blister half-jokingly, two-thirds not.

'I'm not picking *on* him, I'm picking *at* his ideas and opinions. I'm not trying to belittle him or anything. And anyhow, I thought that activists liked to debate their cause. You do consider yourself an activist don't you Miles?'

'Of course he does,' replied Blister. 'We both do, don't we Miles?'

19

This is from *The Washington Post* in 1971,' confirmed Bolts as he squinted at the tablet screen as he wiped his reading glasses on his t-shirt. '1971.'

'Population?' asked Miles cynically. 'Paul R. Ehrlich?'

'It's about an ice-age: It says, **U.S. Scientist Sees New Ice Age Coming**.'

'Oh yeah?'

'Yeah. **The world could be as little as 50 or 60 years away from a disastrous new ice age, a leading atmospheric scientist predicts. Dr. S.I. Rasool of the National Aeronautics and Space Administration and Columbia University says that: In the next 50 years, the fine dust man constantly puts into the atmosphere by fossil fuel burning could screen out much sunlight that the average temperature could drop by six degrees. If sustained over several years – five to ten, he estimated – such a temperature decrease could be sufficient to trigger an ice age**.'

'Fuckin' NASA?' said Bolts.

'That's what I thought,' replied Tilly.

'So, a scientist from NASA got it wrong,' said Miles. 'So what?'

'Yeah,' added Blister. 'So what?'

U.S. Scientist Sees New Ice Age Coming
By Victor Cohn Washington Post Staff Writer
The Washington Post, Times Herald (1959-1973); Jul 9, 1971;
pg. A4

U. S. Scientist Sees New Ice Age Coming

By Victor Cohn
Washington Post Staff Writer

The world could be as little as 50 or 60 years away from a disastrous new ice age, a leading atmospheric scientist predicts.

Dr. S. I. Rasool of the National Aeronautics and Space Administration and Columbia University says that:

• "In the next 50 years," the fine dust man constantly puts into the atmosphere by fossil fuel-burning could screen out so much sunlight that the average temperature could drop by six degrees.

• If sustained over "several years"—"five to 10," he estimated—"such a temperature decrease could be sufficient to trigger an ice age!"

These conclusions—including the ominous exclamation point rare in scientific publication — are printed in this week's issue of the journal Science out today, signed by Rasool and co-worker Dr. S. H. Schneider.

They are also being presented by Schneider at an International Study of Man's Impact on Climate now being held in Stockholm as a prelude to a world environmental conference there next June.

Dr. Gordon F. MacDonald, scientist-member of President Nixon's three-man Council on Environmental Quality, said in an interview that these conclusions point up "one of the serious problems" U.S. and other delegates must address next year.

He called Rasool "a first-rate atmospheric physicist" whose estimate that fuel dust could drop temperatures by six degrees "is consistent with estimates I and others have made."

Whether this could cause an ice age "within five or 50 years or even more," he said, "I wouldn't want to guess."

But he "agreed completely" with Rasool that is is now urgent to start an international network to monitor atmospheric dust.

If his calculations prove correct, Rasool said, it may be simply necessary for men to stop most fossil fuel-burning—use of coal, oil, natural gas and automobile gasoline —and switch in the main to nuclear energy, despite the atom's own disadvantages. Pollution controls alone, he said, cannot, do the job. "I think you have to stop the source."

A new ice age would flood the world's coastal cities and further lower temperatures to build up new glaciers that could eventually cover huge areas.

Scientists have long debated whether man's activity is actually heating or cooling the earth, if either. A "1970 Study of Critical Environmental Problems" concluded that the Rasool-Schneider kind of prediction was impossible to make yet.

"The area of greatest uncertainty," that study concluded, is "our current lack of knowledge" of the optical properties of man-made dust "in scattering or absorbing radiation from the world's largest" fastest comput-

From: *The Washington Post* – 9th July, 1971.

150

20

Tilly took the tablet, checked the battery life and decided to charge it as they read:
She read, '**Space satellites show new ice age coming fast**.'

'When's this?' asked Blister.

'From *The Guardian* this, January 29th, 1974.'

'The opening paragraph to this one claims, **worldwide and rapid trends towards a mini ice age are emerging from the first long term analyses of satellite weather pictures**.'

'I don't recall any mini-ice age in 1974,' laughed Blister.

'Truth is,' replied Tilly. 'We're in an ice age right now and have been for a long time, it's just that there's a slight uptick in temperature in what's known as an interglacial period, which is a time when things warm a little. Officially though, geologically speaking that is, we're in the Holocene Ice Age.'

'**This appears to be in keeping**,' continued Tilly after skipping down to the third paragraph, '**with other long term climate changes, all of which suggest that after reaching a climax of warmth between 1935 and 1955, world average temperatures are now falling. But the rate of increase of snow and ice cover is much faster than would be expected from other trends**.'

They were reporting that in 1974?' asked Miles.

THE GUARDIAN Tuesday January 29 1974

Space satellites show new Ice Age coming fast

By ANTHONY TUCKER, Science Correspondent

WORLDWIDE and rapid trends towards a mini Ice Age are emerging from the first long term analyses of satellite weather pictures.

Of potentially great importance to energy strategies and to agriculture, but barely observable yet in Britain because our weather is strongly buffered by the Atlantic, a preliminary analysis carried out at Columbia University, New York, by the European climatologists Doctors George and Helena Kukla indicates that snow and ice cover of the earth increased by 12 per cent during 1967-1972.

This appears to be in keeping with other long-term climatic changes, all of which suggest that after reaching a climax of warmth between 1935 and 1955, world average temperatures are now falling. But the rate of increase of snow and ice cover is much faster than would be expected from other trends.

The technique employed, which was first described in this country last year during a conference at the Climatic Research Unit at the University of East Anglia, depends on the averaging of information from standard and infra-red satellite weather pictures. In spite of the newness of the technique the findings are important and it is a matter of some urgency that they should be re-examined by other groups.

It is particularly important to know whether the earth's reflectivity is changing, for this is one of the factors in which a change tends to be self-perpetuating until some new worldwide balance is reached. An increase of snow and ice cover coupled with a decrease in cloud, or even with no change in cloud cover, means that more of the incoming energy from the sun is reflected straight out again, thus further reducing temperatures.

The Columbia University findings suggest that at present the main changes are not in the general area of winter snow and ice coverage but in the continuation of coverage later and later into the spring. This appears to be true of both the northern and southern hemispheres.

In the highly complex dynamics of world weather patterns an interconnection of some kind between major events is inevitable, but often obscure. It could be, for example, that the extraordinary occurrence of a stationary low pressure area over Brisbane, with its attendant disastrous flooding, is a feature of the overall trend.

The Brisbane low pressure area appears to have started life as a normal Pacific cyclonic feature moving along a normal south-easterly curving track. But instead of recurving towards the southwest, it was blocked by an anticyclone to the south of Australia. It happens that blocking anticyclones play an important role in the characteristics of weather in the northern hemisphere and account for some adverse changes in our own climate. The trends appear to be cyclic, fairly long-term and extremely important. It is therefore surprising that, in Britain at least, support for scientific analysis of the history of climate is almost non-existent.

But Nottingham at least is fighting off the advancing ice age — grass is growing and seeds are sprouting there now.

The artificial spring has been created by the underground hot water pipes which now carry heat to thousands of homes in the city. As an experiment city officials scattered grass seeds on wasteland near the central library and grass is shooting up there and in other areas where the pipes are.

From: *The Guardian* – 29th January, 1974

'Yep,' replied Tilly. 'They were reporting that there was an increase in snow and ice cover and it was happening faster than expected.'

'And that led so-called experts to conclude that what exactly?' asked Miles with the slightest hint of resignation.

'It led them to conclude that . . .

'Who?' asked Blister.

'Who what?' asked Tilly. 'Who what love?'

'Who concluded? Was this a study or something?'

'It was conducted by two climatologists at Columbia University in New York, Doctors George and Helena Kukla. Says here that after preliminary analysis, the indication is that there was an increase in ice cover across the earth of 12 percent during 1967 to 1972.'

'Preliminary studies?' asked Bolts. 'That doesn't sound too conclusive, if you get me drift.'

'What's the next one; is there another one?' asked Miles.

Tilly handed him the tablet as she stood and inched her way through the short, narrow corridor to the galley where she retrieved a large bag of crisps that she opened and whose contents she emptied in a glass bowl she located in one of the cupboards. 'This drinking's got me a bit peckish.'

'This one's dated June 24th, 1974: From *Time*,' said Miles as Tilly put the bowl in the center of the table and retook her seat.

21

'Crisps?' she asked. 'Help yourselves elves.'

'Can you grab another bottle of wine Bliss?' asked Miles.

Bolts slapped Blister on the backside as he passed and winked coyly but Miles didn't seem to notice and was looking intently at the screen before starting to read: **'Telltale signs are everywhere — from the unexpected persistence and thickness of pack ice in the water around Iceland to the southward migration of a warmth-loving creature like the armadillo from the Midwest. Since the 1940s the mean global temperature has dropped about 2.7 degrees Fahrenheit. Although . . .**

'Dropped?' asked Blister, as he placed the newly opened bottle of Shiraz on the small table next to the crisps.

'Dropped is what it says,' said Miles before continuing: **'Although that figure is at best an estimate, it is supported by other convincing data. When climatologist** *blah-blah*, **areas of Baffin Island in the Canadian Arctic, for example, were once totally free of snow in the summer; now they are covered year-round**.'

'Went on for a few years then this then,' remarked Blister, as he uncapped the wine and coyly, self-deprecatingly so, hand-on-hip, began to pour. 'Can I get anyone anything else?'

Science

Another Ice Age?

Monday, Jun 24, 1974

In Africa, drought continues for the sixth consecutive year, adding terribly to the toll of famine victims. During 1972 record rains in parts of the U.S., Pakistan and Japan caused some of the worst flooding in centuries. In Canada's wheat belt, a particularly chilly and rainy spring has delayed planting and may well bring a disappointingly small harvest. Rainy Britain, on the other hand, has suffered from uncharacteristic dry spells the past few springs. A series of unusually cold winters has gripped the American Far West, while New England and northern Europe have recently experienced the mildest winters within anyone's recollection.

As they review the bizarre and unpredictable weather pattern of the past several years, a growing number of scientists are beginning to suspect that many seemingly contradictory meteorological fluctuations are actually part of a global climatic upheaval. However widely the weather varies from place to place and time to time, when meteorologists take an average of temperatures around the globe they find that the atmosphere has been growing gradually cooler for the past three decades. The trend shows no indication of reversing. Climatological Cassandras are becoming increasingly apprehensive, for the weather aberrations they are studying may be the harbinger of another ice age.

Telltale signs are everywhere —from the unexpected persistence and thickness of pack ice in the waters around Iceland to the southward migration of a warmth-loving creature like the armadillo from the Midwest. Since the 1940s the mean global temperature has dropped about 2.7° F. Although that figure is at best an estimate, it is supported by other convincing data. When Climatologist George J. Kukla of Columbia University's Lamont-Doherty Geological Observatory and his wife Helena analyzed satellite weather data for the Northern Hemisphere, they found that the area of the ice and snow cover had suddenly increased by 12% in 1971 and the increase has persisted ever since. Areas of Baffin Island in the Canadian Arctic, for example, were once totally free of any snow in summer; now they are covered year round.

From: *Time* – 24th June, 1974.

22

'But,' said Miles, 'the main issue is that nobody's listening to our concerns and I'm just afraid, genuinely afraid that we're leaving it too late. Alexandria Ocasio Cortex said three years ago that we only have twelve years left, which means that now we only have nine years before we're over the precipice.'

The New York Times Book Review/July 18, 1976

The Cooling

So writes Stephen Schneider, a young climatologist at the National Center for Atmospheric Research in Boulder, Colo., reflecting the consensus of the climatological community in his new book, "The Genesis Strategy." His warning, that present world food reserves are an insufficient hedge against future famines, has been heard among the scientific community for years—for example, it was a conclusion of a 1975 National Academy of Sciences report. But Schneider has decided to explain the entire problem, as responsibly and accurately as he can, to the general public, and thus has put together a useful and important book.

Schneider quotes University of Wisconsin climatologist Reid Bryson as saying that 1930-1960 "was the most abnormal period in a thousand years—abnormally mild." In fact, conditions of steady, warm weather in the northern hemisphere during that time favored bumper harvests in the United States, the Soviet Union, and the wheat belt of northern India and Pakistan. In 1974 Schneider and Bryson tried to explain to a White House policy-making group why conditions are likely to worsen. One of the most depressing anecdotes in the book is Schneider's description of the deaf ear their warnings received.

From: *The New York Times Book Review* - 18th July, 1976.

'Says the same thing right here,' said Blister, 'at the bottom of this review; says – **"One of the most depressing anecdotes from the book is Schneider's description of the deaf ear their warnings received".'**

Part E: Crisis . . .

23.

'It's all bollocks Miles mate,' declared Bolts. 'They want nothing more than to create what they call a New World Order; they've been yammering on about it for decades.'

'Who's *they*?' asked Miles with a sarcastic laugh intended to ridicule. 'Whenever *they* is mentioned, I can't help but suspect that somebody's about to go off into realms conspiratorial.'

'Yeah,' snapped Blister. 'Who's *they* when they're at home?'

'Those with interests in garnering more power and more control?' suggested Tilly. 'Big business in cahoots with big government?'

'How so?' asked Miles, now suddenly amending his tone to sound less critical. 'D'you have an example?'

'It's like we were on about earlier Miles love; you know, about there being crooked people wanting to profit from war.'

'Yeah: And?'

'And who are those people involved in what for years has been referred to as the Military Industrial Complex?'

'Like you say,' he conceded. 'People in big business that are conspiring with big government.'

'So, you do acknowledge,' asked Bolts, 'that there are people in influential political and/or business positions who are prepared to kill and maim to turn a profit to increase their own personal chances of success?'

'Be careful now,' whispered APONI to Miles. *'I wouldn't trust this guy.'*

'Like I said earlier,' replied Miles as he leant back in his chair, clasped his hands behind his head and feigned an awkward yawn, 'I do yeah.'

'Then why, asked Tilly. 'Why do you find it so difficult to believe that they, people in influential political and business positions, wouldn't organize themselves, or alternatively, simply find themselves orbiting in the same circles as those with similar interests as them to increase their own financial worth, power and influence?'

'Just sounds hinky to me, that's all.'

'Sounds hinky that people in business and/or politics would organize themselves with likeminded individuals or groups in order to succeed?' asked Blister.

'Yeah,' said Miles. 'Does it not to you?'

'But,' replied Blister, 'you just said that you think that it *is* done when it comes to making money out of war, from war profiteering.'

'It's just this terminology that sounds iffy and hinky: The New World Order,' said Miles.

'You've heard of it though yeah?' pressed Bolts.

'Yeah: And?'

'And,' continued Tilly, 'that it, the terminology, has been pumped into the public consciousness by politicians, academics and media?'

'So?' said Miles. 'And.'

'So, let's put aside the terminology for a minute, reset and look at just where and how influential people in business and politics might possibly converge.'

'Go on then,' sighed Miles. 'You know I'm more about the music and less about the politics, right?'

'You ever heard of the World Economic Forum?'

'It rings a bell, why?'

'Well, the World Economic Forum meets up every year in Davos in Switzerland and . . .

'*I've* heard of Davos,' blurted Blister. 'On the news.'

. . . and anyway,' said Tilly, 'every year it meets to hold panel discussions.'

'But what's its purpose?' asked Miles. 'What are they about?'

'Here,' said Bolts. 'Listen to the couple of opening sentences from its mission statement –

"The World Economic Forum is the International Organization for Public-Private Cooperation. The Forum engages the foremost political, business, cultural and other leaders of society to shape global, regional and industry agendas".'

'What's wrong with that?' asked Miles.

'What wrong with an international organization for public-private enterprise?' asked Bolts.

'What?' shrugged Miles again. 'What's wrong with it?'

'I just thought that as a life-long self-described anti-capitalist anarcho-punk, you'd be suspicious of big government and big business collaborating on an international level.'

'Well, who's involved?' asked Miles.

'Says here,' said Bolts –

"The foundation, which is mostly funded by its 1,000 member companies – typically global enterprises with more than five billion US-Dollar in turnover – as well as public subsidies, views its own mission as "improving the state of the world by engaging business, political, academic, and other leaders of society to shape global, regional, and industry agendas . . .

'Over a thousand members?' asked Miles. 'Like who?'

'All the big ones,' said Tilly. 'Like Amazon, Moderna, Facebook, Blackrock, Toyota, Mozilla, Mitsubishi, Manchester United, Pfizer, Deloitte, China Construction Bank and many, many more.'

'I know,' protested Miles. 'But what's wrong with "improving the state of the world" and wanting the best for everybody?'

'Depends on your definition of "improving the state the world" really I suppose,' said Blister leaning his elbow on the table and his chin in the crook of his index finger and thumb. 'Sounds nice enough, but didn't George Bush talk about winning the hearts and minds of the Iraqis and the Afghanis with roads and schools and democracy; Coca-Cola and democracy in place of whatever it is they drink and Shariah Law?'

'So, you,' said Bolts, 'a life-long anti-capitalist anarcho-punk are now suddenly sympathizing with an organization that seeks to merge big business with governments simply because it's tossed out a kumbaya sentiment or two: "improving the state of the world"?'

'So?' said Miles.

'So,' replied Tilly. 'It's like Blister says, didn't the governments of America and Britain trot out similar lines prior to bombing the heck out of Iraq and Afghanistan after September the 11th?'

Miles didn't like the tone of the conversation and the unspoken inference that he had to acknowledge what Bolts was suggesting and what, for that matter, both Tilly and Blister were seemingly agreeing with. He didn't like the tone and the tenor of the conversation, the idea that he had to concede to the notion that he had to object to the idea of an international organization which sought to establish a partnership between public and private entities; an international collaboration between government and businesses. He felt pressured to submit to a position that he agreed with, which was odd when he thought about it.

♭ . *"Stranded: well, I'm on my own . . .*

The problem was Bolts, he was the one turning the screw, forever insisting that Miles clarify himself and making himself look somewhat weak in front of Tilly for opposing his own opinions and defending those sentiments that he despised. He just didn't like the idea of giving-in to Bolts, of looking weak in front of Tilly, and in so defending or seeming sympathetic to the anti-anarchist position of a public body such as a government and a private enterprise in the form of multinational companies collaborating, he'd made himself look stupid in front of everybody. He hated Bolts with a passion, and he despised the influence that he seemingly wielded without much effort. As far as Miles was concerned, Bolts had no intellectual merit and was the kind of punk he loathed: A closet flag-waving patriot who was no doubt against open borders, a real window-licker.

It was obvious, Miles thought to himself, as the other three busied themselves with their phones and commented that this company or that was on the list of partners over at the World Economic Forum's website. He knew all about the WEF and its founder and CEO, Klaus Schaub. Well, he knew of them, not really all about them. That wasn't what concerned Miles; Miles was concerned about the planet and the amount of CO_2 that was being pumped into the atmosphere, the degree to which poison was building up over his head and that of those he loved and loathed alike, Bolts included. Nobody could escape the reality that CO_2 in the atmosphere had increased and that consequently the world was getting warmer, so where was the common sense, where was the sense of urgency and the spirit of togetherness. Where? He asked himself: Where?

'To be honest,' said Miles after rising out of his own circle of thoughts, 'I don't really pay attention to what the governments or the companies of the world are doing because I'm too preoccupied, I suppose, on what they are not doing. And what they aren't doing is meeting the three demands of Extinction Rebellion, which like I've said are: 1. Governments must tell the truth and declare an ecological emergency and 2. Act now to avoid the loss of biodiversity and reduce CO_2 emissions to net zero by 2025 and finally 3. The government must create and be led by a Citizens' Assembly on climate and ecological justice. That's it, it's that simple. I don't care about big companies because I'm against capitalism and I don't care about governments because I'm an anarchist. It's that simple, that's it.'

'But I think we're all, to some degree, sympathetic to anarchism and suspicious of big business and still see ourselves as punks, right?'

Nobody objected to Blister's assumption, yet nobody said anything and instead, each just nodded slightly in the silence as the water outside lapped up against the boat as another vessel slowly chugged by on its way out of town towards Rochdale.

'We have to move quickly,' suddenly said Miles reading from his phone. 'What we do, I believe, in the next three to four years will determine the future of humanity.'

'Who said that?' said Blister.

'Sir David King, former Chief Scientific Advisor to the U.K. government.'

'But you're an anarchist,' replied Blister as he held out his arms, palms questioningly turned upwards. 'You don't trust the government, it's think-tanks or advisors, do you?'

'Not really, no I suppose not. But something must be done. We're definitely running out of time and that quote echoes the way I feel really, says it all. We're almost out of time. Boris said we're a minute to midnight, didn't he? I mean. That's late; that's imminent.'

'It's Tory boy shite,' said Bolts. 'They lie through their back teeth, what with telling us what we can and can't do, who we can and can't meet up with a where and when, while all the time they're doing as they please. Fuck that. You can't seem to rinse the Tory out of yourself can you: bet your folks are Tories aren't they Miles?'

'My mum is, my dad's a Liberal Democrat, or used to be. I don't know what he is now.'

'Yeah?'

'Yeah, no. My mum's a Tory who voted Remain in the referendum and my dad voted Leave, so sometimes I think they just chose to be different in their political persuasions some time back just to irritate each other. That said, Boris, Tory or not, he's right when he acknowledges how late in the game it is, which is all-the-more wonder he doesn't do anything and reach out to us, to Extinction Rebellion and Insulate Britain. I just don't get it if I'm honest.'

'Why do you think he would listen to you Miles, to XR and IB, when he's being pulled at from every direction by countless greatly influential people from around the world? I mean, you're nobody to him and neither are those involved with Insulate Britain who are blocking the roads and preventing people from receiving much needed hospital treatment or Extinction Rebellion who are up to much the same silly antics.'

'Humans are pumping poison gas into the atmosphere which is causing the global temperature to rise and consequently, we and the earth are on what is very soon to be, an irreversible path to oblivion. That's why Tilly, that's the reason why

Boris should be listening to us, why all the governments and companies and individuals everywhere should take heed and listen to our demands.'

♪ - *"The gutter press said punks should spit and fight, and the puppet punks were fooled alright . . .*

'It's like I said earlier Miles mate,' said Bolts. 'It's all bollocks, never mind take heed.'

'Why?' implored Miles. 'Give me one good reason why it's all nonsense.'

'Because,' replied Bolts, 'CO_2 is not a poison and its increase in the atmosphere is not leading us and the earth along a soon to be irreversible path to oblivion.'

'If anything,' interjected Tilly, 'the small increase in CO_2 in the atmosphere and any subsequent increase in temperature is highly beneficial to the earth, biodiversity *and*, people alike.'

Bolts quietly broke the silence that had settled about the table as he reached for his cigarettes and offered them around to his friends while he hummed: 'M-m-m-m-m-m-m-m/m . . . ♪

24

Miles was deeply offended at such talk and even more hurt and now suddenly increasingly emotionally vulnerable due to its source: Tilly of all people. She was the one with the PhD in Ecology and the one who earned a living out of being aware of what was going on in the environment, the one who worked day in and day out with other scientists. How could she blather on about CO_2 being beneficial to the earth, biodiversity, and people alike? It didn't make sense and he felt the sudden need to be alone, to check in with APONI and to reset himself before he said something he thoroughly meant yet might regret.

'And then on top of everything,' said Bolts out of the blue. 'Australian farmers are having to destroy millions of dollars in produce due to lockdowns and meanwhile, guess who's the biggest owner of farmland in the United States eh? M-m-m-m-m-m-m-m/m . . . ♪

'I hope you don't mind,' he said, rising from his seat at the table. 'But I've just remembered that I said I'd check in on Sarah's cats and feed them, make sure they've got enough to drink.'

Although this was untrue, Blister said nothing because it was indeed something that Miles did from time to time for Sarah, who lived just five or ten minutes away from where the boat was moored and who frequently asked him to look in on her pets when she was working nights at the hospital in Halifax.

'Is Sarah working nights again?' asked Blister.

'I think so,' said Miles. 'Unless she's gone back over to Heaton for a day or two.'

'I'm billed to thrits,' replied Blister. 'That she managed to get that job in Halifax after all the trouble she's had . . .

Miles apologized and excused himself, assuring his guest Tilly that he'd be back in twenty minutes or so, half an hour at most. Perhaps because of the wine and the weed, the beer and the now evening's continuing banter, no fuss was made and the remaining three talked on as Miles walked through the chilly evening rain as he dodged the puddles along the path and cursed to himself: 'No good bloody global warming, stupid politicians.'

As he approached Mayroyd he began to regret leaving, wondering whether or not he'd appeared annoyed and therefore somehow "less-than" in Tilly's eyes. He thought he might go and sit on the Wavey Steps for a while and gather his thoughts, see if anybody else was around whose company he could find solace in and put Bolts out of his mind.

'Pay no attention,' said APONI who had been patiently loitering on the periphery of his thoughts. 'It's no use trying to convince anybody of their folly when they're not yet ready for the truth.'

'You're right,' replied Miles. 'It's pointless, utterly futile.'

'Tilly, you know, she's not the same as she used to be, not the same as the days when we lived in Bolton or over in Nottingham when we'd stay up all night speeding.'

'No,' replied Miles, 'I suppose not. Though to be honest, although I'd never really expect anybody to be exactly the same after all these years, it's the absolute ignorance of environmental issues that has me baffled, given her career path these past three or more decades.'

'It's like we've said before though Miles,' said APONI in a reassuring tone. 'True environmentalism isn't an academic issue but one of spirituality; the truth is not always known so much that it's felt. There are many scientists who can't seem to grasp the facts and there are many activists who've never been anywhere near a science textbook who have no difficulty whatsoever in appreciating exactly what needs to be done and the irrefutable fact that it needs to be done now: "NOW!"'

'Now hang on a minute and us a minute will you mate?' Miles suddenly heard before looking up and pulling his hood back a touch so that he could see.

'Pardon?' said Miles to the elderly man who was knelt on one knee, a somewhat embarrassed and shivering Labrador on a leash in one hand and a pink plastic pooper-scooper and a plastic baggy in the other.

'Sorry,' replied the dog-walker with a courteous smile, 'I thought you were being rude and unnecessarily insistent. My mistake.'

'No problem,' said Miles. 'Enjoy the rest of your evening.'

'You too,' replied the man before turning to offer a flash of his eyebrows at the apologetic dog as Miles strode on through the rain.

'Ignore the old man and his dog,' whispered APONI. *'They are fool creatures in the night and know nothing of the earth they are fouling with their existence; they are small and to be ignored. Walk with me.'*

When Miles got back to the boat forty minutes later, he was pleasantly surprised to discover that Blister and Bolts had left, and Tilly was busy tidying up after having done the dishes and separated the empty bottles and cans into different bags that she'd placed just inside the entrance. The place suddenly felt pleasantly domesticated (though not enough to jolt him out of his dank revery) by the calm yet busied movements that Tilly was now engaged in: she'd wiped all the surfaces down, washed the pots, emptied the ashtrays, and lit some jasmine incense.

'Where does the recycling go Miles?'

'I keep the bags of bottles and cans up on deck under a tarp,' he replied with a smile. 'I'll put them up there now.'

'Okay,' replied Tilly, returning the smile as she wiped her hands dry on a kitchen towel. 'Blister got a call from a friend who'd heard that Bolts was in town so the two of them have gone over there for a few beers, said they might be back late, then again they might not. Who knows?'

'They didn't invite you?'

'They did, but I'm a bit too tired for a lad's night out if you get my drift. And anyway, it's raining, and I'd just rather stay in; still a bit jet-lagged I think.'

'It's the carbon,' replied Miles. 'It's the CO_2 in the atmosphere and in the air and everywhere, we're swimming in it, steeped in poison.'

Tilly looked at a still double-masked Miles who appeared to be fretting. He was sat at the table, the thumb of his left hand inserted under the fabric and he chewed at the nail as he scrolled at his phone, before she eventually offered: 'It's not poison love, it's plant food. Well, in increased amounts it might create issues but not as it is right now. D'you know what it is right now?'

'It's a lot, a lot more than it was and what it should be, or so most of the scientists say.'

'What?' asked Tilly. 'Ninety-seven percent?'

'That's an overwhelming majority though, right?' replied Miles. 'Seriously, are you not concerned.'

'About CO_2 and the climate?'

'The weather, the severe weather is what I'm concerned about: The unusual rain outside right now and the change in climate, the increase in temperature and the inactivity of the politicians to do anything to get to net zero and the idiotic mistake of prematurely ending lockdowns. None of it makes any sense.'

'Weather and climate are different,' said Tilly. 'And besides, the rain outside isn't any different than usual, so why does it trouble you?'

'It's different when the climate's changing, it affects everything including the rain. And anyhow, how are weather and climate different?'

Tilly found it a little amusing that despite being so ardent in his beliefs, militant in his attitude and vehement in expressing his position on environmental issues, that Miles didn't know the difference between climate and weather.

'Weather, began Tilly, 'is what's seen or experienced daily and here in Britain can change by the hour. Right now, it's raining but earlier on it was a bit sunny. When we met outside the bank this morning it began to rain. We're on a small island and under the influence of a temperamental weather system, whereas out in the middle of the Pacific, say Hawaii, the weather is perhaps a little less erratic. Basically, climate is weather over time and is measured in spans of thirty years or more. Any period of time less than thirty years wouldn't provide enough data. So, a period, say of one hundred years, would include how many data points?'

'Three?' replied Miles rather meekly after a pause, though with the intent of garnering sympathy and therefore affection as opposed to expressing uncertainty. 'Thirty goes into one-hundred three times, so three data points yeah?'

'Yeah,' said Tilly. 'Three.'

'Okay.'

'Okay. It's often said that climate change is man-made because the global warming began in the nineteenth century when, in England, according to Greta, the Industrial Revolution really kicked off and the burning of coal became more commonplace on an industrial scale.'

'Right,' said Miles, beginning to enjoy the way the conversation was going due to having Tilly to himself without the annoyance of Bolts or, as he occasionally thought of it, the conversational clumsiness of an indecisive Blister.

'Consider The Little Ice Age, which some say extended from the 16th to the 19th century, while others believe that it was from around 1300 to about 1850. Anyhow, the weather between the mid-nineteenth century and the 1930s then began to change and the temperature increased and was far hotter than what we've since seen. So, from the 30s until around 1979 there was a dip in temperature . . .

'Which is when,' replied Miles, 'there were predictions of global freezing?'

'That's it, there were predictions of global freezing and all kinds of catastrophic events to come our way. Then, after 1979 it began to warm a little, concerns about the Ice-Age-Phase were forgotten, and we entered the Global-Warming-Phase. When the temperature dipped slightly again around 2000, we entered the Climate-Change-Phase. Nowadays, it's referred to as Extreme Weather when in fact, there has always been extreme weather events. Note Miles love, note . . .

'Go on, note what?'

'That the terminology that is now used is Extreme Weather, not Extreme Climate. Remember, climate is weather over an extended period of no less than thirty years.'

'Sometimes though, the weather is extremely bad.'

'Extremely bad weather is a noun phrase modified by an adjective whereas Extreme Weather is a compound noun, there's a difference, right?'

'Right, yeah I suppose,' replied Miles, a little unsure of his grammar and whether he'd just agreed to something he concurred with or not. 'Maybe,' he added thoughtfully. 'Perhaps.'

'The terminology just keeps getting changed,' said Tilly. 'And frankly, it's unconvincing. What we've had so far is 1. Ice Age Alarmism from the 50s until around 1980, then we had 2. Global Warming Alarmism from 1980 until about 2000. That was followed by 3. Climate Change Alarmism, and now we're being fed, 4. Extreme Weather alarmism.'

'And you're not concerned?'

'About the weather?'

'Yeah.'

'No.'

'But every time I turn on the T.V. there's somebody talking about how bad things are getting and . . .

'Then don't turn on the T.V. love; look for news from other sources.'

'It's just easier to turn on the television,' replied Miles. 'When it's right there,' he said pointing at the T.V.

'You know, here in England we have the longest running actual temperature records in the world and they go back almost three-hundred and seventy years. The second highest temperature was in 1826 when 17.6 C was recorded, the highest being 17.8 in 1976.'

Nineteen-seventy-six was an important year in the U.K. punk calendar, being that it was the year that the Sex Pistols twice played at Manchester's Lesser Free Trade Hall at the invitation of Howard Devoto and Pete Shelley who were attending the Bolton Institution of Technology at the time. Rumor has it, or maybe it's more like gossip, that many of the future Mancunian musicians had been inspired because of attending either one, or both of those gigs. Of course, there's a lot of northern cynicism too around the two events and it's often said thousands have claimed to have been in attendance, when the actual number was less than a hundred. The year is also memorable because it was when the first punk single was released toward the end of October and on the first of December that year, the Pistols appeared on the Bill Grundy Show and outraged the world, or so the tabloids would claim the next day, with their use of profanity on live television. If it's true, which it's often claimed, that 1977 is year zero for punk and the year of its birth, then 1976 is the year of its gestation, one which is widely remembered because of the binmen strikes, rubbish piled up and the heat. Miles knew that 1976 had been an exceptionally hot year, it was written into punk-lore: Britain was in black and white; the binmen were on strike, the rubbish was piled high, rats were everywhere, and it was really hot.

'Yeah,' said Miles, 'that's right. I remember it being really hot.'

The truth was that Miles didn't remember it being unusually hot in 1976, though somewhere in the back of his mind he recalled watching the documentary *Punk Britannia* where he was sure he'd heard the narrator say things like, "It was a time when Britain was in black and white, the bin men were on strike, the rubbish was piled high, rats were everywhere, it was really hot and punk in England was born in London."

'Right,' replied Tilly. 'And it hasn't been as hot since; not in forty-five years.'

'So why are people saying that catastrophic manmade global warming is an issue, the issue of our time?'

'Why are *you* saying it?'

'Why?'

'Why love? Have you read any books on the subject; do you have any qualifications or training that would strengthen your claims?'

'Of course not,' replied Miles before softening his tone. 'No, no, not like you.'

'So?'

'So why do so many people believe in climate change and . . .

'Extreme weather?' interrupted Tilly facetiously.

'I don't know; really Tilly, I'm beginning to wonder. You know, I don't really know anybody who doesn't believe that catastrophic manmade climate change is the primary concern of our times.'

'But how long has it been your major concern, not just a concern but *the* major concern?'

'I'd say it's been a long time,' said Miles. Quite a long time yeah.'

'But not long ago, wasn't it racism that was the biggest concern and at the forefront of everybody's mind yeah? Racism, homophobia, transphobia, misogynism, xenophobia?'

'I suppose.'

'And only a year or two ago it was BLM, ANTIFA, fuck Trump and the like, right? The media is always serving up some sad scenario or other to keep people tuned in and they must, given that since the dawn of the Internet and sites like YouTube, their audiences are forever dwindling. The BBC and the like, CNN and what not, their audience is shrinking so they come up with fabricated concerns that they cycle into the public psychology and then repeat, reuse or recycle.'

Miles thought for a few seconds and purposely creased his brow before replying: 'Let me check one of my diaries, I've kept a diary since 2000 and I have the last four or five here on the boat, the others are up at the house or over at mum's, not sure.'

Miles got up from the table and went back to the aft of the boat to look around in the storage boxes which were situated inside the bedframe. The mattress needed to be removed as Tilly could tell from the fore-well due to the unnecessary rooting and ruckus that was going on back there and she checked her phone to see if either of the girls in Texas had dropped her an email, suspecting that Miles might be a while. There was no early reason for Miles to look for a diary, but gave her a few minutes to drop each of the girls a brief line to let them know she was safe and sound and enjoying the company of old friends.

25

By the time 11pm had rolled around, Miles had spent a couple of hours alone with Tilly and was feeling pleasantly buoyant, what with the wine, the unexpected calming effect of the weed, Tilly to himself and Bolts now long gone and hopefully never to be encountered ever again. He hadn't been able to locate his diaries but anyhow, he didn't mind being educated by Tilly because she had earned the right to know her stuff, whereas Bolts hadn't, since he'd garnered absolutely no qualifications in science, none. Tilly had calmly said that The Great Pacific Garbage Patch didn't exist and although he'd found that somewhat difficult to believe, she'd shown him satellite photographs in which Hawaii was clearly visible, and yet there was no sign of any floating mound of plastic rumored to be twice as big as Texas or thrice the size of France, it just wasn't there, and he knew why. He knew that it was made up of mostly transparent plastic and was floating just beneath the surface of the ocean, which was why the eyesore was invisible to the naked eye and apparently, to the lens of a satellite camera. APONI had told him that, and he had no reason at all not to believe his butterfly spirit guide: None! Miles cared not to seriously argue with Tilly because he felt sorry for her in a way, her having been conned and tricked, brainwashed in North American universities. Moreover, if that wasn't enough, she'd gone along with the idea of both of her daughters attending universities in Texas of all places: Redneck central and perhaps the last place on earth to have any credibility when it came to scientific integrity, academic merit or just plain everyday common-sense.

It was clear to Miles that APONI was now more of a spiritual confidant than Tilly ever was, though admittedly, the latter had been somewhat instrumental in assisting him to see his true spiritual path. Tilly had been the primary example back in the day when it came to veganism, animal rights and the rights of women and minorities. It was the long nights they'd spent together in her bedsit on Park Road in Bolton, speeding on lines of amphetamine sulfate and coming down with the aid of hashish, Valium and bottles of cider while she taught him about tarot cards, the I-Ching, the importance of personal anarchy and the central tenant of The Wiccan Rede: *Harm none and do what thou will't*, or something like that. In a way, Tilly had been significant, no matter how indirect, in introducing APONI into his life, and for that he was eternally grateful.

Miles suddenly got the urge to lean in and kiss Tilly as she scrolled on her phone and ironically enough, APONI agreed and urged him on, so he did. He pulled his masks aside, leant in and kissed her cheek and surprised, she suddenly turned to face him, and their lips grazed. For a split second he thought that she was about respond with passion but instead, she suddenly withdrew and stood as the door opened and Periwinkle announced her return: 'Ooowee, I'm back: Did you miss me darlings?'

'Where's Bolts?' asked Tilly, as she abruptly stood, making as if she had something to do as she feigned to busy herself while heading to the galley: 'Is there another bottle of wine back here or have we drank them all?'

'He's on his way,' was the reply. 'Said he wanted to go to the shop and would catch me up, meet me back here. It's too cold for a girl to be running errands at this time of the day; excuse me, I simply *must* spend a penny.'

Tilly looked at Miles once Pez had squeezed past and had closed the door to the W.C.: 'What's going on?'

Miles shrugged before reluctantly replying: 'She's been like this for a few months now, a year or so I suppose. I think it's the stress of the coronavirus and the changes we're all experiencing, the uncertainty and everything. D'you know what I mean?'

'No,' said Tilly. 'Not really, no. Earlier today he swanned in here acting all giddy and camp, went back there for a nap, then got up and shaved his head and came wandering in here somewhat more macho with his Discharge t-shirt on having suddenly shed his feminine side. Seriously, what's going on Miles love?'

'Well, she said she was trans a few years ago but in recent months, a year or so I suppose, she's been acting fluid and . . .

'Fluid?'

'Yeah you know, gender fluid. She . . .

174

'He,' interrupted Tilly.

'Well anyway, he or she or they began acting as gender fluid and in recent months has switched between female and male or whatever, many times in the space of a day or less. But I must admit, this is the first time she's shaven her head amid a change from one to the other.'

'Has he seen a doctor?'

'A what?' asked Miles. '*Wow* Tilly. Just wow! Why would she see a doctor? She's gender fluid, not sick and poorly.'

Just then, Periwinkle exited the W.C. and announced that she was going for a lie down in the aft because she was feeling a little tired after her walk, and as the light clicked off in the back, the door at the front opened and Bolts peered inside, 'Anybody home?'

'Come in,' said Tilly. 'We're still here: You weren't gone long, were you? What's going on?'

'I don't know what's going on,' he replied. 'Is he back?'

'Blister?'

'Aye,' he replied. 'Blister, Ray, Periwinkle, Pez. I don't know who I'm talking to half the time. Is he okay?'

'She's fine,' said Miles as he appeared from the galley and entered the fore-well. 'Gone for a lie down, she's tired.'

'What happened?' asked Tilly.

'We were at some house or other and this girl came in with a butterfly tattooed over her top lip, dirty dyed green hair, big boots, face full of piercings and . . .

'Bob,' said Miles.

'Pardon?' asked Tilly.

'Bob. Her name's Bob.'

'Bob the lesbian?' said Bolts. 'With the butterfly tash, an allergy to shampoo & soap, and a face full of rivets?'

'Her name is Roberta,' said Miles, ignoring (the best he could) the ignorance he judged emanating from Bolts. 'Her nickname is Bob.'

'Her's been bobbing and weaving alright mate, dodging the sink and the soap; she wants a fuckin' wash, Jesus.'

'She's doesn't believe in soap,' said Miles. 'She's organic.'

'You can say that again mate; she were well ripe.'

APONI assured Miles, as he made his way to the aft to check in on Pez, that everything was okay and not to worry; everything happens for a reason, even mishaps like Bolts. 'Are you okay?'

'Just tired,' replied Pez from under the covers. 'Though I'm not sure I can sleep, just need half-an-hour to myself.'

Back in the fore-well, Bolts and Tilly were exchanging travel stories and the notion of vaccine passports: 'Texas is pretty cool,' said Tilly.'

'No vaccine mandates?' asked Bolts.

'No, same as Florida.'

'Masks?'

'No mask mandate either.'

'No mask mandate,' echoed Bolts thoughtfully, just as Miles was returning from the aft through the galley and into the fore-well.

'That's ridiculous,' quipped Miles, slowly shaking his head in exaggerated disbelief. 'Don't you think so Tilly?'

'Regarding this pandemic and all the variables that are involved, I don't think anybody really knows what's going on, which claims are credible, and which are not.'

Once again, Miles felt a bit sorry for Tilly, given that she was the one with the PhD and he was the so-called drop-out, the under-achiever living on a rented boat that was financed by the government he despised. APONI reassured him that all was okay and that everything would continue to be fine, that success in the material world mattered not and his concern for nature and the planet made it self-evident that he was morally anchored more that most. Nevertheless, in the silent confines of his private mind he liked to ask APONI for confirmation now and again: 'Really?'

'Really,' she replied as Tilly poured Bolts a glass of wine: 'Claro que si.'

The irritation that accompanied the presence of Bolts was now waning in the wake of his confidence to lean in on Tilly, and he was certain that if Pez hadn't have happened to arrive home at that very moment, she would have returned his expression of affection. Bolts didn't know, thought Miles, just how foolish he looked right now as he chatted away with Tilly, unaware that Miles was ahead of any game when it came to seduction.

'You want some?' asked Tilly, holding up the bottle and tilting it in Miles' direction. 'Or have you had enough?'

'No, no – I can go another.'

'You reckon it's ridiculous then Miles,' asked Bolts, 'for places like Texas and Florida not to push masks or vaccine passes.'

'Absolutely,' replied Miles, as he pulled aside his own masks to take a sip before putting them back in place and continuing. 'Everybody should wear at least one mask in all public places and at home when visited by people not of their own household.'

'A lot of people round here don't wear masks though do they?'

'They don't Bolts, but most do. We decided before so-called Freedom Day that we would continue to wear masks and . . .

'We?' asked Bolts.

'Yes, we. We the community, including the mayor. We get a lot of visitors and for their sake and our own, to show respect and to act for the greater good, residents and shop-keepers decided to continue to wear masks, sanitize and social distance because covid-19 is going nowhere.'

'And the vaccine?' said the still mask-less Tilly, 'Everybody should be double-jabbed.

'Double-jabbed and then a booster,' he replied. 'Or stay at home and self-isolate: play the game and be a team player by getting fully vaccinated or stay at home.'

'It's an easy set of stepping-stones that lead to tyranny,' remarked Bolts. 'I'm not wearing a mask unless I absolutely have to, like on a plane. And I'm not getting any jabs: full-stop.'

'They didn't ask you in the shop to wear one?'

'They did yeah, but I didn't have one.'

'And they still served you?'

'I just laughed and pulled my t-shirt up over my nose. The bloke said that wasn't good enough but after I pointed out that he'd just served a young woman who was using a bandana as a face covering, he just shrugged and that was that, I bought my stuff and left.'

'What are you afraid of?' asked Miles tentatively, feeling a little insecure at suggesting Bolts may feel cornered and come out aggressive, though certain that Tilly would defend him if he were to do so.

'Like I say Miles mate, tyranny.'

'And how can masks and vaccinations which save lives lead to tyranny?' asked Miles with contrived bemusement. 'How?'

'You ever heard of the **Mastercard Wellness Pass** in West Africa?'

'No, have you Tilly?'

'I have as it happens,' she replied. 'I subscribe to a newsletter that monitors what's going on in that part of the world and one or two of them have included articles on what's going on in West Africa.'

'Why?' asked Miles. 'What's going on in West Africa?'

'Mastercard is a technology company, yeah?' said Tilly.

'Right,' said Miles. 'Sure.'

'Well,' she continued. 'Together with GAVI, the vaccine alliance, they have, let me quote here . . .

'Go on . . .

'I'm quoting here,' continued Tilly, looking at her phone –

"Under the banner of "efficiently delivering vaccines to millions of children, tracking identity and immunization records in a digitized manner and incentivizing the delivery of vaccines", Gavi, the Vaccine Alliance – leading partner and catalyst, and Mastercard acting in the capacity of technology partner – have embarked in a Public Private Partnership aiming at deploying the Mastercard Wellness Pass for interested Gavi eligible countries on December 2018. Though major progress has been made in availing immunization in a sustainable manner, one in five children still misses out on routine-life saving immunizations. This partnership aims to leverage state of the art technology by bringing the Smart into the traditional immunization programs for optimal impact in terms of reach, adherence, efficiency and centralized record keeping of children immunizations".'

'I don't get it Tilly, because nothing you've just read sets off any alarm bells to me, does it you Bolts?'

'The Public/Private Partnership wanting to deploy a Mastercard Wellness Pass for interested and eligible countries could be the theme for a concept album for any curious punk band, not that many appear to be these days, at least not the old crowd we're mostly used to listening to.'

'I'm sorry,' said Miles with a tut. 'But I don't agree. 'You sound way too skeptical; what's wrong with helping kids in Africa to get vaccinated?'

'D'you mind?' asked Tilly, looking at Bolts.

'No, not at all,' he replied standing and making towards the galley. 'I'm gonna see if I can find a corkscrew back here . . .

'There is one there somewhere,' said Miles. 'In one of the drawers, I think.'

'The Public/Private Partnership,' said Tilly, 'is an arrangement between governments and corporations, right?'

'Right,' replied Miles. 'Yeah?'

'Yeah, well. Well, the thing is, such arrangements are growing more and more common these days and certain names keep cropping up and . . .

'Here we go,' said Miles, laughing, though more as a means of flirting than with the aim of ridicule. 'Go on: Elon Musk, Bill Gates, the Rockefellers, the Rothchilds, and what's-his-name – Larry Fink?'

'Let's just stick to the facts yeah; you willing to hear me out?'

'Go on then,' said Miles, enjoying seeing Tilly backed up against the ropes so to speak, about to attempt to defend conspiracies nobody on Earth had a chance of viably housing. 'I'm all ears.'

'I can see that you're doubtful Miles, and I don't blame you. The thing is, I doubt it too. But some things are undeniably true and therefore worth paying attention to and . . .

'Such as?'

'Such as GAVI. If you look on the GAVI website, you find this –

"The Bill & Melinda Gates Foundation: Gates Foundation pledged US$ 750 million to set up Gavi in 1999. The Foundation is a key GAVI partner in vaccine market shaping".

'So Gill Bates and his wife set up a vaccination foundation in 1999 and pledged a shit-load of cash, so what? Good for them.'

'Philanthropy and using vast wealth is a good thing right?' asked Tilly.

'Of course,' replied Miles. 'Absolutely.'

'And philanthropic capitalism?'

'How d'you mean, philanthropic capitalism?'

'I mean that he's been known to say that vaccines are phenomenal profit makers, with more than a 20 to 1 return. In a few short years, he almost doubled his wealth from 50 odd billion dollars to over a hundred billion dollars, and that was well before the coronavirus pandemic.'

'Are you sure?' asked Miles, brow creased, face scrunched, in an attempt to persuade Tilly that he was growing somehow sympathetic to what it was she had to say. 'I'm not convinced.'

'Me neither Miles love, me neither; but it's worth checking out, don't you think?'

'Well, what else? Okay, he invested three quarters of a billion dollars in vaccines and he's reportedly said that vaccines are a good investment that yield a 20 to 1 profit, right?'

'Right.'

'Then what else?'

'He invested in GAVI which aims to, let me get it right: Hang on a sec Miles love, I'm looking on their website . . .

'Okay, take your time.'

'Right, it says here, it says −

"Gavi also works with donors, including sovereign governments, private sector foundations and corporate partners; NGOs, advocacy groups, professional and community associations, faith-based organisations and academia; vaccine manufacturers, including those in emerging markets; research and technical health institutes; and implementing country governments."

'What's wrong with that Tilly? I don't get it; I don't understand what you're driving at. Seriously, what's your problem?'

'The concern that many people have is that several things are beginning to converge, and some say that the result will not bode well for the future of humanity, regardless of the philanthropic rhetoric surrounding current events because all this do-goodery could just be a Trojan Horse, a wolf in sheep's clothing. You see, not only does Mr. Gates believe that the moral imperative to ensure that huge sums of money find their way to places like Africa and that he has stated that investment in vaccines yields vast profits, he is working with companies like Mastercard to create what is referred to as a Wellness Pass that is presently being used in West Africa and that appears to be being championed in many other parts of the world since the advent of the corona virus and the push for universal vaccinations, or should I say, repeated and ongoing universal vaccinations.'

'If people are sick,' replied Miles, 'and need vaccinations, then what's wrong with him supplying vaccinations? Really, we need people to be jabbed right now and he's doing a good job, don't you think?'

'Traditionally, vaccines are administered before a disease is circulating in any given population, not after it's gained purchase and is spreading and mutating. A lot of epidemiologists believe that introducing a vaccine, a new one at that, could well possibly create more harm than good in the long run.'

'Then why would a vaccine be introduced?' asked Miles. 'Seriously Tilly, you don't really think that Boris and Joe and Bill and whoever else is involved, are aiming to kill millions and reduce the population like the rumors going around on social media are claiming, do you?'

'No,' replied Tilly. 'Of course not, no.'

'Then what?' implored Miles. 'What?'

'What people are beginning to question is what looks like a serious conflict of interests. He and his friends have so much money and power and their vision for the future has been outlined and published. Let's quickly summarize yeah and . . .

'Go on then,' said Miles, reaching for his tobacco tin.

'Firstly, he and his wife, or ex-wife, set up a foundation and started GAVI, the vaccine alliance. Secondly, he donated so much money to the World Health Organization that only the U.S. and the U.K. gave more money in 2018 and Trump later withdrew American funding, so Gates potentially has clout, right?'

'Right,' replied Miles. 'Maybe, I suppose.'

'Thirdly, Gates has invested in vaccine manufacturing companies which right now are turning huge profits. I mean, who the hell made Bill Gates an epidemiologist? It's like Al Gore telling us all that the world temperature was rising and that as a result the polar ice caps would melt, sea levels would rise and coastal communities would be destroyed, then he went and bought multi-million-dollar beach-front property and we're supposed to sit back and take this guy seriously? I mean, seriously Miles, are you buying that?'

'I'm just worried about the world, concerned for the environment. Aren't you?'

'Aren't you what?' asked Bolts, appearing from the galley.

'Concerned about the environment,' said Miles. Worried about the world.'

'Not me,' said Bolts. 'You Tilly?'

'I have concerns,' she replied. 'Industrial pollution, waste management and such things, but not about global warming or extreme weather events, no.'

'And the coronavirus?' asked Bolts.

'Of course,' replied Miles.

'Not at all,' shrugged Tilly. 'Not for myself at least. I'm concerned that it may affect older, more vulnerable people, or people with underlying health issues, but I'm not really concerned for my own personal safety.'

'You're not concerned about any of this Bolts?' asked Miles. 'Really?'

'It's a can of worms Miles mate in my book: we've got global cooling and a coming ice-age, the ozone layer, global warming, climate change, and extreme weather events on the one hand, and on the other we've got a corona virus and the actions of global bodies around the world and politicians of every western country telling us that we need to lockdown, socially distance, mask-up, shut-up shop, don't travel, don't visit relatives and friends in care homes, stand on the doorstep and clap and applaud, get a jab, get two jabs, get a booster. Meanwhile, a lot of these politicians who are handing out directives left, right and center that are backed with law enforcement personal dressed up like fuckin' Robocop and the bloody Terminator aren't even following their own rules. People are frightened to fuckin' death of their *external* environment in the form of weather and climate; rain, sleet, snow, wind and sunshine, and they're scared shitless of their own *internal* environment and every cough, cold and sniffle they encounter, each runny nose, ruddy cheek and sneeze they come across and folk are confused, so they toe-the-line and go along to get along. They've been fuckin' hypnotized pal. Meanwhile, small family-owned businesses are contracting and collapsing while huge multinational companies are expanding and seeing unprecedented increases in profit, right? And anyhow, how come this virus can get past two vaccines and a booster but not a thin paper mask? I'm going along with none of it until they get their stories straight, and that's that.'

'I see your point,' conceded Miles. 'But, none of it's been orchestrated right, nobody would manufacture such a scenario. I mean, businessmen are just . . .

'Businessmen are what?' giggled Tilly. 'You Miles, an anarcho-punk, lifelong anti-capitalist are going to defend the collaboration between big business and government?'

'But are they collaborating?' asked Miles. 'Are you sure they're colluding and in cahoots?'

'You don't think money talks?' asked Tilly.

'I dunno,' mused Miles. 'I suppose: Maybe.'

'Maybe?' asked Bolts.

'Are you two picking on him again?' asked Pez, suddenly appearing with a yawn, and taking the final fourth seat at the small table. 'What are they badgering you about now Miles?'

'We're talking about the environment and the pandemic and whether or not big companies are collaborating with governments.'

'To what end?' asked Pez. 'Why would they collaborate?'

'Exactly,' said Miles. 'To what end, why?'

'The bottom line?' suggested Tilly.

184

'Money?' asked Miles.

'I can't believe that anybody would ever think of making enormous amounts of money by lying or warping the truth about the climate catastrophe or the pandemic nightmare that we're facing,' said Pez, lighting up a cigarette. 'Nobody would do that; not for no amount of money or influence, nobody.'

'What about your Discharge t-shirt mate?' replied Bolts.

'What about it?'

'Almost every song they've ever bloody written is about the horrors of war and

. . .

'And what have the horrors of war got to do with money?'

'You're joking!' said Tilly.

'No, I'm not.'

'What was the Gulf War about then?'

'Oil,' said Pez, before adding, 'Okay, oil for the sake of money.'

'You agree?' asked Bolts. 'That there are those in governments around the world that start wars for profit and influence under the guise of national defense or the defense of allies yeah?'

'Yeah, yeah,' said Pez. 'Yeah, I get what you're saying.'

'And you Miles?'

'Same: yeah. Unfortunately, there are those in positions of power who will sacrifice the lives of others to make a profit or create a legacy for themselves of some sort. Yeah, I can agree with that.'

'We talked earlier right, about war profiteering?'

'Right,' acknowledged Miles. Like I say, I can agree with that.'

'And,' suggested Tilly. 'Given what we were looking at earlier, you know, the newspaper articles and all the scaremongering that was going on in the 70s about the imminent encroachment of the Big Freeze, do think it's at all possible that politicians, academics and some in the business sector now are bending the truth to meet their own needs and that catastrophic manmade climate change or extreme weather events or whatever, are similarly more scaremongering tactics than undeniable fact?'

'Media cunts too,' said Bolts. 'Them scabby twats are in on it too; shit-bags, 'kin job-lot of 'em.'

'What d'you think?' asked Miles, looking at Pez.

'I think that tilly might have a point, thinking about it. If politicians and people in the military industrial complex will collude to make money or create a legacy or go to war to better their own situation, then sure, why wouldn't people lie their arses off about the weather for similar personal gain? And you?'

Miles thought for a moment before conceding: 'I think you're right Pez, though it's hard to actually accept. It's difficult to fully wrap your head around the idea that some people will, behind the scenes, engineer wars and conflicts so that they can acquire wealth or status or legacy or whatever.'

'Right then,' said Tilly. 'We all agree, I think we all agree, that there is such a thing as firstly, war profiteering, and secondly, climate profiteering, yeah?'

'No doubt in my mind,' said Bolts.

'Same here,' added Pez.

'Me too yeah,' Miles admitted. 'Me too; but where are you going with this? I can see your brain ticking Tilly.'

'I know,' said Pez. I know what she's getting at.'

'Go on then,' said Bolts. 'Spit it out.'

'Well,' Pez continued. 'If we can acknowledge that there are people in this world who organize and engineer wars for profit and that there are those who would manipulate data and use, what I can only describe as psychological warfare, or at the very least psychological manipulation regarding the climate or weather or both, then . . .

'Psychological warfare?' scoffed Miles. 'Do you . . .

'Let him finish, said Tilly. 'Go on Pez; then . . .

'What I mean is,' continued Pez, 'is that if there are war profiteers and climate profiteers, then it wouldn't be too much of a stretch to suggest that there are pandemic profiteers, because I'm damn sure somebody, somewhere, is making a shit load of money out of all this two jabs and a booster malarky, and that the idea of even more boosters will be touted once or twice or more next year.'

'Ta-da!' exclaimed Bolts as he raised his arms in the air like a center-forward having executed a successful penalty kick in the 95th minute. 'Nail on the head lad, bang on. Thing is mate, several folk (including Tony Blair) have suggested the need for a fourth and Turkey has made a fifth one available for some people.'

APONI was ruminating somewhere in the deeper recesses of Miles' mind, he could feel her wanting to say something, and then she did: *Ignore him Miles, he's a proper Charlie, addle-headed and spent, and I'll tell you what'll come next . . .*

'What next?' asked Miles. 'I mean, if that's true – though to be honest I'm highly skeptical – where do we go from here?'

'You're only skeptical mate,' replied Bolts, 'because you're nice.'

'Because I'm what?'

'Because you're a good person who finds it difficult to comprehend that there are folk in this world who'd ever contemplate manipulating so many people to acquire any kind of personal gain. You're just too nice, or maybe naïve and not too widely travelled, to appreciate the levels of evil that there are in the hearts of men.'

'Hearts of men?' laughed Pez. 'Very poetic Bolts.'

'Well, you know what I mean. There are some right cunts knocking about.'

'You're right,' replied Miles. I do find it difficult to believe that there are individuals who would even think of doing such things for money or any kind of personal gain, let alone think it through, plan it out and execute it on a global scale after colluding with others.'

'Listen to this,' said Tilly looking at her phone: '"The individual is handicapped by coming face-to-face with a conspiracy so monstrous he cannot believe it exists. The American mind simply has not come to a realization of the evil which has been introduced into our midst. It rejects even the assumption that human creatures could espouse a philosophy which must ultimately destroy all that is good and decent".'

'Who said that?' asked Miles. 'Ronald Reagan?'

'That was J. Edgar Hoover, first director of the FBI, born in 1895 and died in 1972.'

'Read it again,' said Miles. 'That first bit about face-to-face.'

'"The individual is handicapped,' read Tilly, 'by coming face-to-face with a conspiracy so monstrous he cannot believe it exists".'

'That's you Miles,' said Bolts with a teasing laugh, before changing his tone of voice to that of a cartoonish arch-villain. 'You're too nice to be able to believe that anybody could ever come up with such a dastardly plan.'

'I told you we'd have him,' whispered APONI. 'I knew he was weak, and he would bend and break and wind up handing out undeserved compliments.'

'Undeserved?' Miles silently enquired. 'You think he's playing me?'

'I think he's weak,' she replied. 'I think we have him beat.'

'Can we trust him?'

'Who can you trust?

'I can trust Tilly.'

'Can't.'

'Can.'

'Can you do me a favor Miles,' asked Tilly out of the blue, looking at her watch. 'Only, it's getting late, and I still haven't heard back from Frances, so it looks like I might have to stay here, is that okay?'

188

'No!' demanded APONI. 'It's NOT okay.'

'Of course,' replied Miles. 'I've told you already, of course you can stay.'

'Shit me,' said Bolts. 'What the fuck?'

'What?' replied Miles. 'You can stay too if you want Bolts, I didn't mean to be ignorant.'

'No mate no, it's not that, but ta anyroad, thanks. It's this here: Mensi's dead.'

'That's weird,' said Tilly. 'We were only talking about him earlier, weren't we Miles?'

'We were yeah.'

'Sad that,' said Pez. 'Proper sound he was.'

'What did he die of?' asked Tilly.

'Covid's what it says.'

'Was he jabbed?'

'Fuck knows,' said Bolts. 'But, being a big lad the size that he were, you can bet your back teeth his doctor would've recommended he get jabbed and boosted.'

There was a short silence as each of the four let the penny fully drop, personally acknowledged the departure of yet another somewhat like-minded soul: A man who was always vocal about the role of the police in what many viewed to be an ever-increasingly destined authoritarian society. It was once a bit of a game to rebel against the system and The State, to question its motives and express distrust, but it was no longer just a game. No longer was saying 'fuck the system' just a t-shirt slogan to differentiate yourself from the normies and the straights, the indoctrinated hivemind that was everywhere, that which offered little other than bread and circuses for many, life on the dole, football on the telly, noon-time meals of pasties or Pot-Noodles and a chippy tea on Friday.

'It wouldn't surprise me,' said Bolts. 'If he had been jabbed and boosted, what with the way the vaccine is being screwed into everybody's head as the only solution. I mean, have you seen that compilation on YouTube of American T.V. show sponsorships: "Brought to you by Pfizer, brought to you by Pfizer, brought to you by Pfizer." These shitheads are making money hand-over-fist and to label them Pandemic Profiteers is not hyperbole, not one bit. Read an article the other day that pointed out that BioNTech, Pfizer and Moderna are making a combined profit of $65,000 every single minute from their, and I now quote, "highly successful" COVID-19 vaccines. That's over a thousand dollars a bastard second, and no wonder it's "highly successful" when folk the world over are coerced and blackmailed into getting three fuckin' shots apiece. Successful? Aye, successful alright when it comes to making money for selfish shit-weasels.'

'But wait,' said Miles. 'I'd like to go back to this Mastercard Wellness Pass in West Africa that was mentioned earlier; what exactly is it?'

Tilly scrolled at her phone, cleared her throat with a cough and said, 'This is from Privacy-International-dot-org –

"Public-private partnership launches biometrics identity and vaccination record system in West Africa

In July 2020 a public-private partnership program between the Bill Gates-backed GAVI vaccine alliance, Mastercard, and the AI identity authentication company Trust Stamp was ready to introduce a biometric identity platform in low-income remote communities in West Africa. The program will integrate Trust Stamp's digital identity platform into the GAVI-Mastercards "Wellness Pass", a digital vaccination record and identity system powered by Mastercard's AI and machine learning technology, NuData. Critics are concerned that the program is more aimed at promoting the health of markets for vaccines and Mastercard's "World Beyond Cash" program rather than the health of individuals, and that it provides an excuse to expand the use of biometrics in national ID registration systems, and note that Trust Stamp is offering the same technology to COVID-19 response that it offers to law enforcement and prison systems for the purposes of surveillance and predictive policing."

'I don't want to sound skeptical just for the sake of it Tilly,' said Miles. 'But, the thing is, every time I hear the name Bill Gates in relation to vaccination, biotech or AI I can't help but put whatever is being said into the realm of conspiracy theory.'

'It seems less like a conspiracy,' said Pez. 'And more like collaboration; a business venture or something.'

'Like I say,' said Bolts. 'Between private and public: government and business. Collaboration between friends is often the grounds for business in some cultures, I'm thinking of China. Guanxi, or connections, is widely practiced and is in and of itself a kind of currency. For example, I lived in a comparatively small town between two large cities, each a dozen or so hours away by train. The train from Beijing to Xian stopped at several places along the way and each town along the way was allotted a certain number of tickets depending on the size of the population and the projected demand on any particular day. Anyhow, I had to go to Xian a couple of times a year, but I couldn't just show up at the ticket office and buy one because communist party members who worked at the station would commandeer them and sell them to people that they knew as a favor: demand for tickets was always higher than what the station could supply. Sometimes the face value would be inflated, but more often than not, they would sell them at the regular price or give the tickets away, in the understanding that the recipient was now indebted. My boss at the collage found it easy to get tickets because he was in a position to influence college entry, test scores and party membership. If the guy at the station with the tickets had a friend of a friend of a friend that had a son or daughter who wanted to enter the college, he could rely on my boss to wave the would-be student through whereas other potential students, no matter how bright, would be denied entry. Everybody wanted guanxi, or connections; friends with influence who had other friends with influence, who in turn had associates who had resources that could be accessed.'

'And?' asked Miles.

'Yeah,' added Pez. 'So what?'

'Well, the same thing happens in other circles: there are old boys' clubs everywhere, especially in politics and business. The World Health Organization is funded by several countries and organizations, including The Bill and Malinda Gates Foundation and GAVI, which Bill helped to found. Rich people use their resources to acquire more resources, right?'

'But didn't' he give a lot of money away, you know, like half his wealth or something?'

'He did Pez,' said Tilly, 'But he doubled his billions and more in the space of a decade. He bought influence, including donating nearly 320 million dollars to media organizations to gain favorable coverage. He bought good P.R.'

'Well, if there are people in governments and business who are working together, what're they working towards?' asked Miles. 'And don't say New World Order.'

'It's people in business and politics that have been using that term for some years now Miles love, there are several compilations on YouTube from George Bush senior to Justin Trudeau in Canada stating that a New World Order will emerge, though they don't always us the same language. These days, politicians and influential people in business and tech tend to talk in terms of Build Back Better.'

'Right,' said Pez. 'I've heard that phrase a few times: Build Back Better. Where did that come from?'

'We mentioned the World Economic Forum earlier, right?'

'Yeah,' said Pez.

'Right,' said Miles.

'Did,' said Bolts.

'Well,' said Tilly. 'I'm not really sure exactly where it comes from, though I think its origin lie in the idea of building back better after natural disasters like the 2004 Indian Ocean earthquake and tsunami. Remember that?'

'Yeah,' said Bolts.

'Right,' said Miles.

'Did it really?' said Pez.

'It's a phrase that's been used many times since,' added Bolts, 'by many outfits, including the World Economic Forum. The covid-19 pandemic is seen by some as being equivalent to a natural disaster because it has damaged societies around the world in many different ways. Earthquakes and tsunamis damage physical infrastructures, but they also create many other types of problems such as inflicting psychological harm and distress, the disruption of the economy due to the disruption of supply lines and such yeah?'

'Yeah,' said Pez.

'Well,' continued Tilly. 'In 2016, the founder and executive chairman of the WEF published a book titled, *The Fourth Industrial Revolution* in which he outlined emerging technologies.

Bolts and Internet yarn.

'Hang on a sec,' said Miles. 'Fourth Industrial Revolution.

'That's what I was thinking,' added Pez. 'What were the other three?'

'The first, replied Tilly, 'was the steam engine and mechanical production. The second was the advent of the assembly line and mass production due to electricity, and the third was the development of computers and the Internet.'

'So, what's the fourth?' asked Miles. 'I don't get it, what is it?'

'It's really wide ranging, but in essence, it's about emerging technologies and connectivity.'

'The Internet of Things,' said Bolts cynically. 'And people as data.'

'What?' asked Miles.

'Yeah,' said Pez. 'What?'

'The Internet of Things is a thing,' laughed Tilly at their incomprehension. 'Right Bolts?'

'Right, it is. The Internet of Things is basically a humongous network of things and people connected to the Internet sharing data. These new emerging technologies include all types of things that will be connected to the web, including shite like your fridge and your car, your coat and your front door.'

'Your coat?' said Pez.

'Yeah, your coat. Well, at least what is termed as the "Wearable Internet" which could manifest in many ways.'

'Like the Apple Watch?' asked Pez.

'Like the Apple Watch,' replied Bolts. 'Though in theory, it could be in the lapel of you shirt or your coat and could be connected to you fridge and your car and your bank and your job and your local government and your national government and global institutions like the World Health Organization and its affiliates who will be able to deny you access to all manner of goods and services if your medical status is not up to date and your browsing data illustrates that you have been attempting to access questionable information.'

'Questionable information?' queried Miles.

'Yeah, you know, like things which are not approved of.'

'Sounds like paranoia to me.'

'Doesn't to me,' said Pez. 'There are loads of things these days that are considered questionable and are frowned upon, that are not approved of.'

'Such as?' said Miles.

'Such as questioning the vaccine. I mean, like you Miles, I've had three, but I don't want any more?'

'Really?' replied Miles. 'Why?'

'Because we were told we needed one, then it was two, then three. Now in Israel they're talking about a fourth while in Turkey they're on about a fifth. I smell a rat: I'm calling B.S. on this Miles.'

'No wonder they're laughing,' quipped Bolts, though nobody thought to ask why.

'A silent weapon,' said Pez. 'For a quiet war: Chinese bio-weapon. B.S.'

'Why d'you think it's bullshit?' asked Miles. 'You didn't think it was B.S. when you got your booster; when we got our boosters.'

'Yeah Miles, I know. But the thing is, they keep changing the goalposts, don't they? They lull you into compliance with the promise that if you get one jab, you'll be able to get back to normal but then it ends up being three or four or more and there's still no real proof that we'll ever get back to normal.'

'You're suddenly talkative aren't you?' said Miles. 'What's got you going?'

'What's got into me? I'll tell you what's got me going I will: Bullshit. Most of us have been pumped full of B.S. over the past nearly two years and I'm just about done with it Miles, aren't you?'

'*Mutant thoughts,*' whispered APONI to Miles. '*Distorted views.*'

'There is an element of distortion,' replied Miles. 'But don't you think it's for all our sakes?'

'There are too many inconsistencies,' interrupted Bolts. 'Too many things that don't make sense, far too many clown-world events. I saw this clip of a woman buying coffee in a drive-thru but the male employee wouldn't hand the customer her drink because she didn't have a mask, but said he could provide her with one. Of course, she just laughed and asked, "So you can't give me my drink because I'm not wearing a mask, but you can give me a mask and once I'm wearing it, you can then hand me my drink?" The guy confirmed that that was the case and she asked him why he couldn't just hand her the drink if he could hand her a mask, to which he answered, "I can't hand you the drink because you're not wearing a mask, but I can give you a mask and once you've put it on, I can then give you your coffee." That's fuckin' stupid and reminiscent of the first experience I had in this whole shit-show. I was entering a restaurant, nowt posh, just your average café type place and the woman at the door told me that I had to wear a mask and that if I didn't have one, she could give me one. She gave me one and I put it on and walked to our table, a journey of less than ten seconds, and then once I was sat at the table, I was permitted to remove it. I was also free to move around the place to go to the water station or the toilet. It was daft

195

as fuck and made no sense, but as far as I could see everybody was simply complying as though it was the most natural thing in the world to be doing.'

'I think it just cuts down the apprehension,' replied Miles. 'Makes people feel more at ease and safe.'

'You call it apprehension Miles mate,' clipped Bolts. 'I call it fear, and I suspect that to some degree, it's been manufactured. You see, there's this doctor who presents a show each day that reports on what's going on around the world with covid. His focus is on statistics and to begin with, I was under the impression that he was pretty much neutral. Then, Omicron came along and despite the doctors in South Africa who first identified it as a new strain and were in the thick of it saying repeatedly that although it spread faster than the Delta variant, and that the symptoms and overall impact that it had on people who contracted it was much less severe, his tone was full of alarmism. He went over the main symptoms: slight cough, sore throat, sneezing, headache, and tiredness. Then he had the gall to say that the symptoms were so benign that if you did catch it, you might just think that it was a cold and not bother to get tested and that's not the way you should think about it, you should get tested.'

'He own shares in any particular brand of testing kit?' laughed Tilly. 'Or just chumming the waters with clickbait?'

'No idea, but I tune into his channel once or so a week to see if he's still peddling the same brand of fear, and he usually is.'

'And anyway Miles, you've then got former covid-19 adviser to Biden, that's epidemiologist Michael Osterholm, coming out on CNN and admitting that the type of masks worn by the vast majority of people are ineffective against coronaviruses despite orders from the CDC to wear them. That's bollocks mate, plain and simple, dogshite.'

'Why would the Center for Disease Control tell people to wear masks if they are useless?' asked Miles. 'Seriously: Why?'

'Why Miles?' said Pez. 'Seriously? Even I know the answer to that.'

'Go on then, why?'

'To separate us, to divide and conquer and to . . .

'Atomize us,' interrupted Tilly. 'To break us down and build us back up like they did after 9/11. Things, regarding international travel, never got back to normal after nine-one-one did they?'

'No,' replied Miles. 'You're right there, they never did get back to normal.'

'I was going to say control us,' said Pez as she reached out and touched Tilly's arm. 'But yeah, I think atomize us is probably the right word; split us up into tiny pieces so that we look to authority figures and big media for direction, because like it or not, that's what people have been doing for almost two years.'

'People will think nothing in a few years from now love, you know, about wearing masks and providing proof of vaccinations and then . . .

'Then,' broke in Bolts. 'Then the technology will change, and it'll be a chip or . . .

At this, Miles let out a sudden bust of ridicule-tinged laughter and instantly felt like he may have crossed a line with tin-snipping Bolts, but he needn't have done because Frank simply gestured to Miles in a manner that invited him to elaborate: 'It's the idea of people having to get chipped: I'm sorry, but it just sounds way too much like a conspiracy.'

'And I take your point,' replied Bolts. 'I take your point. Too be straight up, I don't think there is the need to coerce people into getting chipped, they've been doing it voluntarily in Sweden for a couple of years. If the coming wave of implantable technologies were simply advertised as lifestyle accessories, fashionable next-generation tech to be desired and highly sought after, people would readily accept them. However, there seems to be a sinister hue surrounding implantables, that is creating resistance and rebellion. And, I suspect that this resistance is being manufactured so that the State can claim to justify a harsher approach to managing any type of civil rumblings, however they are defined. And we know how innocuous incidents and use of language can be manipulated by the State to claim the right to intervene where they have no business at all, no legitimate claim of jurisdiction.'

'Like what?'

'Like the police contacting people and handing out cautions because in an online thread they've said something along the lines of transgender women, that's male to female, not being able to lactate and feed an adopted baby.'

'Well, said Miles. 'Just because a transgender woman can't feed an infant doesn't mean it should be pointed out.'

'Even when the baby is at risk from being under nourished because this sick cunt insists on sticking his man-tit in the kid's gob in the hope that he'll suddenly be the first ever bloke to be able to successfully breastfeed? The issue is the State redefining what is morally right and acceptable and then using that newly created standard to proclaim that it has the right to interfere in peoples' lives.'

'Maybe,' said Miles thoughtfully. 'Yeah, maybe.'

Bolts once again hummed the same familiar sounding tune to himself, 'M-m-m-m-m-m-m-m/m . . . ♪

'It does seem at times,' said Tilly, 'that the public (the world over) is in many places, being goaded into acting violently. Especially in places like Australia. I can't believe what's going on in Australia. I mean, comparatively, they don't have much of a problem with covid-19 but the response from the authorities has been way more over the top than you would ever have expected to see down-under. Prolonged lockdowns, travel restrictions and coppers dressed up like Robocop. S'hard to fathom at times.'

'Boris insists that testing is one of the most important lines of defense against covid,' said Pez. 'But, the thing is, I don't really trust him and think that he's a stooge. I'm sure he was the shoo-in that broke the Red-Wall over Brexit so that he could appear more believable to the working-class when it comes to following the mandates on masks, social distancing and vaccines. Somebody, somewhere, has got some dirt on him, some real shit-lips nasty crap that he'll do anything to avoid coming to light. I'd bet my boots on it.'

'A lot of propaganda going on: fuckin' stacks. Smart cities, fourth industrial revolution, emerging technologies and what not all being touted on the back of a virus that most people survive. Paid off media, corrupt politicians and what not; these big pharma outfits that's making loads of money have our best interest in mind? Pull the other one.'

'Does it not bother you at all?' asked Miles. 'The virus?'

'Does it fuck. I'm not even sure that it exists,' replied Bolts before again humming the same tune without looking up, the same repetitive riff: 'M-m-m-m-m-m-m-m-m/m . . . ♪

'Not at all?'

'No. And all this mask business is little other than managing perceptions and maintaining anxiety and fear in the general public; now it's jabs that are separating people and not masks. Go to the supermarket and stand in line at a distance, don't trust that the people around you can't harm you with their very presence. What's coming next eh? Lockdowns due to concerns about the climate? Carbon tax? Fuckin' plant-tax: plants which intake CO_2 and output life-giving oxygen that people can't do without?'

'"Modern man,' sang Miles to himself, quoting one of his all-time favorite punk band, Bad Religion, '"Pathetic example of earth's organic heritage, just a sample of carbon based wastage, just a tragic example of you and I . . . ♪

26

It wasn't long after that everybody had decided that they'd had enough for the day, so after a couple of last joints of hashish and cleansing ale apiece in the form of *Stella*, each found their spot for the night. Blister or Pez or Ray or Bliss or Periwinkle went to bed first after wishing the others well with a - 'Tight-tight everybody, sleep night.'

The following morning Miles awoke shivering to discover he was onboard alone and aimed to try the bank again because after meeting Tilly on the previous morning, he'd left the queue and the two of them had shared the umbrella back to the boat. After a quick trip to the toilet where he pissed and puked, he sat on the bed looking around for his socks as he reached for his jeans, though before pulling them on, he finished off the half glass of red wine that was on the floor next to the overflowing ashtray. On the fore-well table lay a note from Tilly explaining that she'd woke-up cold, hungover and couldn't sleep. She'd finally got a message from Frances, and they'd arranged to meet up early and go for a walk, maybe catch the sunrise. The tone was breezy and light, with the mention that it would be good to catch up again, time permitting, before she went back to see her girls in Texas. It ended with her signing off with a cute little heart next to her name and beneath that in block letters written in a different color of ink were the letters: PTO.

On the other side of the sheet of paper was a post-it note, one of his own from an almost expired pad that he kept affixed to the fridge door with a magnet shaped like Buddha. The paper was blue and in the bottom right-hand corner was a laughing emoji. Miles and Pez used them to inform each other of their comings and goings and to suggest what they may have to eat on any given evening, or whether or not there was any weed stashed on the boat for the other's use while one was away at a friend's place. Steve Ignorant written on a post-it note meant that the weed was under the sink in the galley, whereas Pete Shelley indicated that there was a rolled joint slipped inside the pillowcase on the bed in the aft, notes of that nature.

Miles couldn't quite recall what time he passed out, but he remembered lying in bed listening to Bolts and Tilly wind down the evening and how it annoyed him just listening to Bolts and the crap that he came out with, the possibility that he'd inured

Tilly with his bullshit and hardened her attitude toward the current situation. The very thought that she could become in any way as indifferent to the planet and the pandemic as Bolts riled Miles and he rattled around impatiently in one of the cupboards until he found a small brown bottle of 5mg Valium: he took one and put a second in the small pocket of his jeans as he called to mind what had irritated him so much. Not only had Bolts repeated his disregard for the existential threat to the planet, but he'd also brazenly doubled down on the fact that he wouldn't be getting vaccinated, no matter what. Miles was concerned that Tilly would be influenced and decide that she and her daughters would decide not to keep up with their jabs and end up ostracized. It wasn't just the refusal to respect the threat to the environment though, or to get vaccinated; it was the whole blasé attitude, his socio-pathic indifference to practicing social norms. Bolts laughed at the idea of wearing a mask or even allowing anybody to take his temperature with a pistol shaped thermometer pointed at his head because in his words, "it was a slippery slope to tyranny when you surrendered to people pointing such things at you day in and day out before you could enter a building, or have a series of shots or you'd be out of a job or banned from attending classes".

He told Tilly that he thought it was idiotic to socially distance and stand on certain spots (as indicated) on the floor in shops or banks and such like, wear a mask or to use hand sanitizer. The lack of responsibility, thought Miles, was unfathomable and as selfish as anything he'd ever come across. Why couldn't Bolts just knuckle down and get with the program, accept that sacrifices had to be made?

The last thing he remembered hearing as he lay awake, drifting off to sleep, was Bolts introducing some video or other that he said Tilly might find interesting: 'I think a lot of people feel the same way to be honest Tilly.'

'You think?'

'Sure, though most can't really get away with speaking out about the situation we're in, not on social media or on the mainstream media.'

'Right,' said Tilly 'I know.'

'Then there's Rogan on Spotify who can say whatever he wants, his podcasts getting something like ten times the number of listeners than his mainstream detractors.'

'I know who he is,' replied Tilly. 'But I've only ever had the time to listen to one or two of his podcasts. He's a comedian, right?'

'He is yeah. Anyhow, have a listen and see what you think.'

"It really is almost as though we're being attacked. They're just mandating that people do this one thing, one size fits all. When they're saying that, when the unvaccinated shouldn't have access to health care, what they're doing is signaling to their tribe, the people who also took the vax, the good people. They feel this way: we're gonna fight off the outsiders, we're gonna deny them health care, fuckin' cast them out of society. It's what happens when cowards encounter adversity. When cowards encounter adversity they give in quick. They give in quick, and they decide that what they are doing by giving in quick is virtuous. There's also very clear influence, of both the media and of the politicians, by these massive pharmaceutical companies. If you wanna talk about the most criticized and the most disparaged aspect of our society when it comes to like the dangers of peoples' health, that the desire to earn unstoppable and constantly ever-growing amounts of money every year, well the big one is pharmaceutical companies. Forever we've been suspicious of these people, forever people have pointed to them as being one of the real problems with capitalism that mix with medicine. And here's my biggest fear; it's an engine for controlling the population, it's an engine for the institution on some sort of social credit system. We give into that sort of surveillance over here, the government will be watching every goddamned thing you do, and I think that's coming."

What had really annoyed Miles was listening to Bolts pontificate about how although America was bad in ushering in totalitarianism, Canada had been worse and Australia even worse still, and that the country to reverse the alleged trend toward a global technocracy, would be England of all places. He yammered on about how England had ended the trans-Atlantic slave trade, and then had been an example in extricating Britain for the European "political" Union, and that it would be England that would lead the world out of this, what he termed as, this march toward a global technocracy.

'Ha,' thought Miles. 'Cheap-shit, crappy little old England: as if.'

∞

Miles passed out after that, and here & now . . .

𝄞 – *'Slow, slow, quick-quick slow,* sang APONI. *'No telling me what you don't know . . .♪*

. . . stood in the queue at the bank waiting to check his accounts at the cashpoint to see if his dole money and rent had come through, he noticed that the same overweight security guard as the previous day was monitoring the line as it glacier-like advanced toward the machine, before realizing that it wasn't a security guard at all but a silver-haired man collecting for charity. He couldn't help but laugh at himself and then felt a sudden pang of concern, as the familiar sensation of an encroaching panic attack hit him because *after all* he thought to himself, there ought to be a guard making sure that social distancing was strictly observed. Moreover, he'd heard that the masking mandate was about to be lifted and that people would be free to come and go without face-coverings which some people celebrated as a sign of returning civil liberties, though Miles was doubtful that he would readily ditch the habit come late January because he wasn't sure that he was yet ready to embrace that degree of personal indulgence.

He then then switched his train of thought to stave away the discomfort and began to wonder whether Tilly had taken her poster with her, the black and white Poison Girls poster that she'd said she liked so much. He hoped that she'd forgotten it in the haze of a certain hangover rush to leave and meet up with her friend Frances, so that he'd have an excuse to contact her and maybe secure the chance of seeing her again: she'd *friended* him on Facebook yesterday, he had a way of contacting her. He was thinking of Tilly and the poster, trying to recall whether he'd seen it as he was leaving just twenty minutes ago or so, but he couldn't. As he stood, craning his neck this way and that to gauge how many people were in line in front of him, a tune emerged in his mind and repeated itself over and again. Then it dawned on him, it was the same nine syllables that Bolts had kept sarcastically and provocatively humming: M-m-m-m-m-m-m-m/m. It was a song about freedom Miles recalled, something about freedom. As he stood in the queue at the bank thinking about Tilly and her girls and if, in the near future, they'd be fully vaccinated and safe to go about their young lives, free from the worry of any new and yet undetected variant virus, the words to the song slowly seeped into his consciousness . . .

"Why do you think that they are laughing? That was it, wasn't it? That was the tune that Bolts kept repeating: M-m-m-m-m-m-m-m/m - **Why do you think that they are laughing?**

🎼 Because they've got you where they want you –

They taught you fear of falling, they taught you
Fear of feeling, they taught you fear of
Freedom . . .

🎼 *Fear of reason,* interrupted APONI with a laugh -

Fear of freedom,
Fear of freedom,
Fear of freedom,
Fear of freedom . . . ♪

出口: Exit/Epilogue

"People who refuse to accept vaccines, I think the right response for them is not to force them to, but rather to insist that they be isolated. If people decide, 'I am willing to be a danger to the community by refusing to vaccinate,' they should say then, 'Well, I also have the decency to isolate myself. I don't want a vaccine, but I don't have the right to run around harming people.' That should be a convention," said Chomsky.

"Enforcing is a different question. It should be understood, and we should try to get it to be understood. If it really reaches the point where they are severely endangering people, then of course you have to do something about it," he added.

Speaking on YouTube's Primo Radical on Oct. 24, Chomsky said that for the unvaccinated people who are segregated from society, how they obtain groceries should be left up to them. "How can we get food to them?" asked Chomsky. "Well, that's actually their problem."

- *National Post,* **October 27, 2021**

*

"From the first night we were told to lock down I realised I was more frightened of authoritarianism than death, and more repulsed by manipulation than illness."

— Laura Dodsworth, A State of Fear: How the UK government weaponised fear during the Covid-19 pandemic

*

Future pandemics will be far worse than Covid: Speaking about the work done by CEPI, the Microsoft founder said in a statement: "As the world responds to the challenge of a rapidly evolving virus, the need to deliver new, lifesaving tools has never been more urgent."

- Bill Gates.